DIGNITY

KEN LAYNE

This is a work of fiction. The characters, situations, organizations and events portrayed in this novel are either products of the author's imagination or are used fictitiously.

Desert Oracle Books

P.O. Box 1735, Joshua Tree, California 92252

www.DesertOracle.com

books@desertoracle.com

First Paperback Edition: May 2011

ISBN: 0983559821

ISBN-13: 978–0983559825

This book is for Jesse and Harrison,
in hope that *some of it* comes true.

1

To my brothers and sisters at Shadow Vista Estates,

It is raining in the desert and has been for many days now. A dozen little rivers roar down the hillside and the canyon, tearing at the roots of juniper and cactus, and sending the jackrabbits and ground squirrels running from their flooded burrows.

Come springtime, these sodden brown hills will explode in color and blooms under a clean, clear sky — and the violence of the winter will be forgotten. May the same be true for all of you.

I am well and go unnoticed in this place. There's a woodstove and your letters to keep me company. What first felt like hiding, I now appreciate as an opportunity to dwell on B and all that has happened and all that will come in the future.

You say it is difficult to write a letter. Because you can't tap out a message on a phone that whispers your secrets to our persecutors? Don't cry for things we can no longer keep. We are wary now, but we are alive. Were you alive in the past, spending all your time staring at a screen?

B gave us many things, but one of the greatest gifts was breaking us free from phones and screens and the false idea that we had friends because the phones and screens said so. How many of those friends turned on you after B was taken? How many poisonous people from your past life — your work or your school or even your own family — were fast to call the police?

Because of what? Your words, your thoughts, your giving to those who had nothing? Because in B you saw a way of life that held dignity and meaning in a world that had become cheap and tawdry?

"Mostly we are still shocked," you write. "We don't have much else to talk about and some of us are depressed. How can we remember B in a way that is not so sad?"

Here is what you should do: Be cheerful, and celebrate your time with B.

Each evening meal is a new chance to live the way we desire, with food of our own making, together at a table with conversation and fellowship. We raise our glasses and say, "To B, who is with us still." And then, "We honor this food, we honor each other, we honor our Earth, we are patient for Justice."

When the meal is done, do what B did and walk in silence and contemplation, for one hour. You are all lucky, to be at the edge of the wilderness in the evenings, under the charging sky and sea of stars.

But we can take steps even when we're trapped in an apartment with the unmarked car outside, or confined within a jail cell. We can contemplate all that is good even if our limbs are bound and our eyes covered in the prison hood. The day approaches when we will all walk in the light of day, when police and soldiers clear our path instead of hunt us down. Be patient.

What did B say on his last day? "I am alive, and I am free."

You are alive, and you are free.

N

Please pass this letter on, if you can, to our brothers and sisters in Alamar Crossing and Riverstone. My greetings and good thoughts go to them, too, and I will write to both communities before I next see our messenger.

2

To my dear friends at Covington Spring,

Your letter arrived a week ago, safely delivered by Eli on his way to Pinyon Peak, and I've kept it with me as I walk and reflect on the lives you are living and the courage you show.

"Our community is growing here," you write, "despite everything."

Despite everything? Your community is growing *because* of everything. It grows because your beliefs are true and your hearts are pure. But remember to show the same wariness that B would show to those who showed interest in our ways of living. Not only are the police and government informants endlessly trying to infiltrate our peaceful communities, but the turmoil and great need of our times will make many converts of convenience.

Keep newcomers at arm's length until they've shown the sincerity of their beliefs and the goodness of their souls. Do not turn away anyone who is hungry or needs a night or two of shelter, but reserve a place in the community only for those who leave no doubt that they belong with you.

How long should a new brother or sister or family be considered a provisional member of the community? Six months seems reasonable, as that gives the chance for fellowship and conversation with them, and the chance for them to show they will share in the community's responsibilities and live in peace with us. Think of Yarrow, and all B fulfilled there in a half–year's time!

If the person is not appropriate for us, or if their family is too torn or troubled to be in harmony with the community, give them two weeks' time to move along and see that they are well supplied for their journey. If they will not leave of their own will, cut them off completely from the community — our food, our water, our fellowship — until they go away. Choose carefully who you allow inside the community and these problems will be few. What did B say when that motley gang of disturbed people arrived at Yarrow in their monstrous campers full of motorcycles and angry dogs and giant televisions?

"We have no more room here, but if you leave all this behind I will go with you today and help you start a community of your own."

And they turned around and drove away.

Thank you for your happiest news, about the new young couple expecting a baby. The first child born at Covington Spring! B knew this day would come, and I can only wonder if he knew it would come so soon after he was taken away.

N

3

My friends in Goleta Meadows,

I think about you always and honor the sacrifices you make for our community.

How is our little group? Are people from the area still showing up for the weekly suppers? Keep your gates open to neighbors, and hide nothing from the honestly curious. We are living without the three poisons by choice, to show the world a new path, in fact a new map of the world. Don't be weary. Don't rob yourselves of music and conversation and laughter!

It saddens me that Salvatore and Jane have left us. Why did they leave? I can't answer that. Maybe it's *because* they were the last in your community who knew B. Think of all the questions the newcomers must have, the expectations that those few who lived and worked with B somehow take his place.

You write, "And now we try to live up to what B wanted for us, and not one of us ever saw B face to face." Maybe that makes it easier. I knew B as well as anyone could, and I often stare at the blank page wondering what to write to our scattered communities.

But I will tell you a story that you can tell the others.

After B was set free from the Los Angeles county jail, those who remained loyal to him gathered at the home of Vera and Tommy in Echo Park, that crumbling old cottage that looked ready to topple down the hillside. We shared a meal around their great wooden table. The blinds were closed because already the unmarked cars were clumsily parked outside and the spies were watching from the street. The table was lit by two great candles and we were about to begin when the garden door flew open and B ran in, laughing, because he was forced to go through the alley and over a fence and then jump down to the garbage cans below and the knees of his pants were ripped and dirty.

We embraced him and he looked at us and said, "This gloom is intolerable. If you can smile and enjoy each other's company, sit down with me. If not, go outside and scowl at the policemen."

Then he led us in a song and we filled our glasses and he said, "Honor this food, honor each other, honor this world that is our home."

Someone, I can't remember who now, started crying and said, "But what will we do?"

B smiled in the candlelight and helped himself to the food and passed the dish to me, sitting at his left.

"What will we do?" He took a bite and answered, "We are already doing it."

N

4

Dear friends at Mariposa Landing,

Just writing the name, Mariposa, fills my mind with memories of your village there in the oaks, sharing in the happy labors of your little farm and watching your children play in the foothills.

I hope things are as they were, although I fear unpleasant changes may have occurred since I last sat at your table. It has been a very long time since I had a letter from you.

But your last letter is still with me, and for the time being I am at Elora in this lonely stone cabin with the corrugated tin roof. When it rains, which is rare, the sound on the roof is outrageously loud, like a line of marching drummers. It reminds me of summer thunderstorms pounding the rooftops at Yarrow.

You asked for my memories of Yarrow, stories you could tell each other and tell the children. Here is one I don't believe I've written down before, perhaps because I've heard it told so many times that I forget how much time has passed since it was told again.

B had decided we would leave Los Angeles, that it was no longer safe for any of us — and he was right. Vera and Tommy did not feel the urgency and that was the last time we saw them. But the rest of us walked down to Alvarado Street and waited in the darkness of an alley behind a gas station while B went brazenly down the sidewalk waving at taxicabs. One car finally stopped for him and he stuck his head inside and then it sped off. We didn't know what this meant and began to panic. But B came back to the alley and asked, "Where are you running to? Aren't you coming with me?"

We stepped to the curb just as a yellow taxi van pulled over and the driver got out to help us inside. Somehow all nine of us crammed in and I saw B put a clump of twenty dollar bills in the driver's hand. It was strange to see him use money.

I fell asleep somewhere along Interstate 5 or Highway 14, with Jane's head on my shoulder and my face pressed against the cold glass of the back window. When I woke, the taxi van was bumping along a two–lane road somewhere in the Mojave, through the shadow shapes of Joshua trees with their great spiny branches reaching into the night.

B was whispering to the driver and then we were stopped at a private road cut off by two lines of concrete roadblocks. I followed the others out of the van and stood there drowsily in the wind. B encouraged us to follow him, the high half moon and the stars our only illumination. The road ended at a single rounded block of half–finished new houses.

We chose one and unrolled our sleeping bags on the bare floor, the nine of us in a circle, and I was asleep again in minutes. The sun blasting through the uncovered windows brought me back to life a few hours later. B was nowhere to be seen.

In the light of day, we saw our camp was an abandoned new housing tract. Only our rounded block had houses, while the neighboring block had concrete foundations with pipes sticking out from unbuilt bathrooms and kitchens, the rest of the land mostly undisturbed except for a grid of empty asphalt streets and cul–de–sacs that went on for about a mile.

"It will work fine," B said with a grin when he returned later that morning.

We tried to share his enthusiasm but almost immediately began bickering about the lack of food and water, and the scorpions skittering across the floors while we slept, and the black widow spiders hanging in the corners from their sticky webs. Celia yelled that it was all foolish.

"You don't just drive out to the desert and pick some random place and expect us to go along with that," she shouted.

B took her aside and the rest of us stood around awkwardly in the shade of the garage doorway. They returned in a while and B said, "Who will go with Celia to turn on the water?"

This is how the work began, without any direction or plan said out loud. The taxi van returned that afternoon with sacks of bulk groceries and then left again with Francesca and Robert, in search of house tools and garden tools from yard sales. A week later, the cab driver returned again, this time with his wife and little daughters and their belongings in suitcases and supermarket bags. All of this happened with Javier, the driver, translating for his wife and babies. We showed her to a house and she cried, I didn't know if from joy or horror. The little girls played all day in the patch of wildflowers and sand outside while their mother made a home of the barren house.

In that first week, a truckload of dirty second–hand solar panels appeared, and then another truck arrived with a load of rich soil. Celia, our engineer, managed to turn on the water main to the housing tract at a setting meant only for testing the system for leaks. It was plenty for our little village of twenty houses as the water piping had been designed for hundreds more homes that had never been built.

The water lines bothered Tobias and he said so, complaining about the injustice of the aqueduct from the Sierra Nevada, about people living where they shouldn't live. B smiled and said, "Would you go back through Egypt and Rome and tear down all traces of irrigation, too?"

Some of us laughed and B rested on his shovel and said, "We have the will to choose between culture and civilization."

N

5

To my patient brothers and sisters in Mariposa Landing,

Forgive my delay in writing. I have quit the cabin at Elora. I was finally noticed here and I probably stayed too long. They wanted to see what was on my desk and bookshelf. They upended everything but found nothing that would interest them. But it was the signal to move on, and I managed to slip away into the desert.

A set of railroad tracks cuts across the wilderness there, and I came across a haunting scene that night as I waited for the freight train making its way up the steep Kelso Grade. Parked here and there by the tamarisk and desert willows were battered little pickups, with groups of men crouched in the darkness. To the southwest I saw the bobbing light of the first locomotive, and once the line of four straining engines had rumbled by and I scrambled through the sand and gravel to find a handhold on a freight car, these groups of shadowy figures were already hopping onto the train, moving rapidly up the ladders and onto the rooftops of the cars, in a loosely coordinated raid.

As I wedged myself between two cars, I saw boxes falling to the ground as the little trucks pulled up and the pirated goods were hurriedly loaded in the back. On the south side of the track, I watched the shadow figures of children slashing at other boxes in the half moon's light, knocking aside the ones of no value to them — a carton of stuffed toy bears, another of red-white-and-blue basketballs.

Let me return to a happier tale, the settlement at Yarrow.

That spring flew by, with all of us delighted in the work and especially delighted by the place we were creating. I had thought there was nothing uglier, nothing less humane than the ghastly stucco housing developments at the farthest edge of the great Western cities. They sat out there divorced from town and nature both, connected by new roads to new concrete clusters of supermarkets and electronics stores, with plastic lighted signs over the entrances as the only decoration. For twenty or thirty years they continued to grow outward, propelled by a mysterious momentum, until it all suddenly stopped — until it all stopped and the people realized the momentum had been not only the cause but the entire purpose.

And yet here, upon the skeleton of a charmless housing tract abandoned after the crash, we had built a place of community that was open to the sky and stars and desert foothills. The largest structure — a gargantuan obscenity that could've sheltered fifty people but was designed for perhaps five — B designated as the common house.

As in all the unfinished houses, we had roofed over this one's exposed two–by–four rafters with sheets of green corrugated metal liberated from outside a scrapyard in Victorville This gave the little village the cheerful look of a forest camp for schoolchildren, and was so pleasing to the eye because it was so very different from the concrete red tile that adorned everything in California from fast food restaurants to mental health clinics.

Inside the common house, all windows and glass patio doors had been left uncovered, leaving the big rooms not only filled with sunlight but filled with the view of the mountains rising up to the south. With its sparse furnishings and clean concrete floors and makeshift copper bells in the huge kitchen where we cooked for everyone, the vulgar exurban mansion was as serene as a Japanese temple.

In many of the houses, the huge attached garage had the only exposure to the sun and mountains, and in those cases we made the garage the main living room. Our water and our electric ovens were heated by the sun's power. After dark we used lamps fueled by the oil of the jojoba bush, and the nighttime hours were restored to their quiet mystery.

Because of the peculiar street design of the housing tract in those last years, our small community consisted of three circular cul–de–sac pockets within a single curving island of houses surrounded by the Mojave. The small front yards of the houses were ideal for the gardens, close enough to one another to attract bees and conserve water and make the work exceptionally pleasant because it was done alongside your neighbors, with children playing between the plots. With our compost and borrowed water and desert sunshine, the crops grew quick and plentiful.

We rose before the sun, walking a path that looped around the low hills. There were birds to count and coyotes to admire. After breakfast, we worked until the midday meal, and spent the heat of the afternoons reading or talking or napping or sitting on the floor of the common house staring out at the mountains and Joshua trees. In autumn and winter with daylight more scarce, we would work after lunch, too.

Work has never been the right word for what we did at Yarrow. It had nothing to do with the kind of work I had done before meeting B, before so many of us were dismissed from our strange routine tasks at computer desks and construction sites and office parks. Ishiko said once, as we weeded the vegetable rows on a breezy afternoon, "I used to rush home from the office to get some time in the garden before dark. I was just doing my work in the wrong place."

How did we escape notice for so long? We were quiet, and there was no automobile traffic to or from our little neighborhood. There were no telephone calls to trace, no mail or packages to call attention to our unnumbered houses. Among all the abandoned housing tracts and foreclosed suburbs of the Western states, with their plagues of theft and methamphetamine and vandalism, Yarrow was invisible. The concrete barriers still blocked the entrance road.

B came running back at twilight one evening to say he'd seen a mountain lion stalking through a sandy wash just behind the common house. He began to walk that arroyo's length every afternoon and that's what ultimately led to his second arrest.

N

6

To my dear friends at Cabernet Ridge,

I received your letter yesterday, and it filled me with happy visions of your farm and your community. When things have quieted down, it would be my honor to visit you there and help in your fields and celebrate at your table.

You ask about the beginning of our undertaking, how it was that we — city people frantic with neurotic worries and money hustling and hunger for diversions to entertain our bored minds — created Yarrow and then spread out to help begin the many other communities.

You ask if we had a plan. Perhaps there should have been a plan!

B, of course, acted as though everything was part of a beautiful pattern revealing itself as we went along. Whatever unspoken grand design may have existed in his mind, chance and coincidence seemed to dictate our actions. "Seemed," I say, because I could be completely wrong about this. If the eight of us often felt baffled by what was unfolding around us, B took particular delight in what he called "curveballs."

This is how it began in Echo Park. First, there were the dinners. We had been friends, some of us, for several years by that time — from college or the office or playing music together or walking dogs in Griffith Park or just from living around each other. In this way we were no different from those privileged adults of extended adolescence once common to the great cities. But, being that it was Los Angeles, we spent much of our time simply driving to jobs downtown or Santa Monica or wherever our work required us to be. It was the usual insanity of a place with little in the way of public transportation and its rare affordable housing far from the jobs.

The dinners and drinking we once did at an old neighborhood Mexican restaurant had been lost when that little place closed down — to make room for a designer clothes shop that barely lasted a year. We said good–bye to couples who were moving away with their new babies and those who went off to new cities. It seemed we might fade away from each other, down our separate roads of busy work and banal complication, when B returned from a backpacking trip somewhere and said, "We are letting our lives slip away."

No–one could argue that. And so, that very week, we began the weekly meals. We brought something, each of us, whether a dish or a bottle or a book to read from. It was unspoken that we would not turn on the screen, that this was a time to be alive with one another and not to stare at an entertainment flickering on the wall.

It was B who brought a garage–sale straw basket one night, to Vera and Tommy's ramshackle bungalow stacked atop that dubious cliffside held together by ice plant and ivy. He placed it by the door, where a coat rack might stand in colder climates, and shook us all down for the phones and other electronics in our pockets and purses.

He asked, "Who enjoys talking to a head bowed down to an iPhone?" We laughed and he dropped in his own device, and when one or another of them began beeping and ringing during the meal, he leapt up and hid the whole basket away in the linen closet, behind a stack of blankets and towels.

With just that, just the lack of those things blinking and bleeping, we gained a few hours' peace during that weekly meal. And within a few months' time, the weekly meal had become twice and then three times a week. And when the cost of the fruits and vegetables from the farmers market grew too high in the winter months, B led us after the meal one evening to a narrow vacant lot between a simple old cottage and a tall concrete dwelling that had been built just the year before. Speculators planned to build an extravagant dwelling on the sliver of land, but the collapse was beginning and the financing had fallen through.

"It faces south," B said, pointing out the charms of the dirty lot in the streetlight glare. "It will be a beautiful garden." The builder's sign was already half–covered in graffiti and the hard dead earth was littered with hamburger wrappers and cigarette butts and shards of glass liquor bottles. The sole of my shoe became stuck to the ground and when I tugged my foot up, I saw a used condom hanging from the sole.

"We'll need to clean it up just a bit," Celia said through a scowl.

On that next Sunday, we cleaned it up. The new house to the east was unsold and still vacant, we learned, while the old place to the west was inhabited by two very old gay men who barked insults and threats at us throughout that first day. Nothing happened, of course — the police wouldn't get out of their patrol cars in Echo Park unless there was an actual body on the ground — and when the angry old couple finally realized we had cleaned the lot and painted over the gang names, they let us alone and eventually even offered their water hose once we arrived with Tobias' little pickup truck loaded with rich black soil.

Now, I didn't have the slightest clue what a garden involved. Like most of us, I had only begun to pay attention to food in recent years. My childhood consisted of frozen inventions warmed in a microwave and processed meals from fast-food franchises or the "casual dining chains" reserved for special nights out. In college I ate burritos stuffed with greasy bits of meat and finally learned to scramble eggs in my apartment. But one day, without knowing exactly how or why, I was aware of what went on the plate. Just using plates was part of that little awakening, as it seemed most food was being consumed from paper wrappers balanced between bellies and steering wheels.

How insane it all sounds: First we wanted to eat fresh food that didn't make us feel sick, and next we were literally running for our lives, the police and the government at our doors and then at our backs. But that is getting ahead of things.

B was spreading sheets of newspaper on the cracked dry ground and then spraying a mist of water on top, a technique he picked up from a gardening magazine, and then we were all doing this, making a little grid of wet newspaper rectangles. The soil we dumped in rows over the newsprint, and over that we made lines of dried manure that smelled earthy and rich. From the great mounds of mulched Christmas trees left by the city beside the Los Angeles River channel, we had piney wood chips to spread around the rows. The biggest cash investment was about forty dollars in organic seeds — lettuce, tomatoes, squash, Brussel sprouts, melons, cilantro and sage and parsley and herbs of all kinds, and exotic greens like kale and bok choy, collards and Swiss chard.

Not everything came up, until we learned to start things inside, in cardboard egg cartons on the windowsills. The clever city squirrels got most of the lettuce before we became clever enough to cover their favorites with chicken–wire domes. And until Celia insisted we liberate some sections of collapsed chain–link fence around an old gas station on the corner, we kept losing the crops closest to the street to people using the lot as a parking spot.

But in time, in what seemed to me an amazingly brief amount of time considering my complete ignorance when it came to the basic mechanics of growing plants for food, we had a farm. Neighbors, mostly Latina women who had kept gardens before coming to the United States, began asking if they could use a part of the lot, too. And so the garden became a community garden, meaning that the garden created a community — our first community. Our neighbors, the crotchety old men, never set foot on the lot. But they became our scarecrows, and we found no more broken glass or other garbage on the soil.

Meanwhile, our meals became festivals — feast days, which is what *festival* means. Vera and Tommy lived around the block from the garden, so their house became the common house, their vast wooden table our community table. When Tommy was laid off — such a weak, degenerate term for being thrown away by the machine's managers — he joyfully went to work on the bungalow, doing all the little projects he'd never had time for, opening all the windows to the peculiar Los Angeles sunlight, cleaning away the clutter, and assembling a great pile of unwanted plastic and clothing and electronics in the tiny single–car garage at the bottom of the cliff.

Asking Tobias for an afternoon with the pickup truck one evening meal, Tommy said he needed to give the stuff away. B asked where he would go, and Tommy said he didn't know, a thrift shop or something.

"Across from the garden is that concrete lot," B said. "Why not bring the things there, and let people take what they want?"

And that is how the shop was born.

N

7

To the brothers and sisters at Adobe Terrace,

You ask me a difficult question: What is the ideal community?

I have not seen a community that is ideal — even within our movement, there is no single ideal that encompasses all of that which brings us peace and delight in living. And a community is, at best, a flexible framework for lives that are in endless change and motion. Even the brother or sister who lives in tranquility in a bucolic village will face disappointments, the loss of family and friends, illness and death. So, let the ideal of your community not be too idealistic! Let it serve you as a refuge from the parts of the world we've turned away from, and as a bridge to the true earth we embrace, and let it be the sturdy shelter that stays close at hand on your journeys through this life.

Now what I *can* tell you is that we are lucky to have such fine and varied communities, and there are dozens I have visited within California and a few I was able to visit before it became difficult to get across the state line. Your ideal could be and should be different from mine — in matters of preferred climate or architecture or any such variable, everything is necessarily slanted to an individual's taste. The desert is my home and I feel welcomed by the scorching sun and tough thorny plants and the idiosyncratic wildlife with its scales and fangs and horns. But water is scarce and many find the landscape too naked and brutal.

We have brothers and sisters in the Sierra Nevada who would be out of sorts if they weren't still slushing through snowbanks in May, and communities in the Northwest where three seasons of relentless rain is exactly what they expect. There are builders who love river rock and deplore adobe, and cooks who consider a meal incomplete unless they've plucked fresh mushrooms from the sodden ground. And then there was B, who personified those who spend the different seasons in different locales, so that one could swim and surf and spear fish in the ocean during the summer months, and ski from house to house in the wintertime, and pick apples from the mountain orchards at harvest, and work in the soft sunlight amongst a riot of wildflowers in the deserts at Spring Equinox.

The fact that so many of our communities are in the California desert is one of those accidents of fortune that B so loved. It was his belief — not just his, but the belief of enlightened people throughout our short human history — that the desert offered something distinct to those seeking clarity and working toward wisdom. Unless spoiled by the droning buzz of the off–road motorcycles or the dreary monotony of shotguns fired at beer cans and junked appliances, the deep quiet and vast space of the deserts demand that our babbling brains be stilled, that we breathe in the clean dry air and feel the immensity of existence.

What brought the property speculators to our deserts had nothing at all to do with a mediation on the severe beauty of the desert, of course. It was simply the farthest fringe of the metropolis, where the land was cheap as far as borrowed dollars go. That these distant abandoned tracts were the final heavy burden on their worldwide house of cards was utterly unknown to these so–called developers, as they raped the desert crust and crushed hundred–year–old tortoises asleep in their burrows and toppled the ancient Joshua trees and scraped the ground clear of yucca and cactus and blooming brush.

But in their dumb greed, they left us the physical framework of our first communities. All the things we sought — solitude, nature, the reuse of existing structures, the space for our gardens and our souls to grow unmolested — we found in these vulgar, hideous housing tracts dumped upon the desert as if dropped from a helicopter. Where they saw failure, in the untouched desert they could not destroy because they were ruined by their own desperate bankers, we saw nature preserved in every direction. And so the *ideal* was in fact a series of blunders and misfortunes that only became that ideal — our ideal — when we opened our eyes those first bright mornings at Yarrow and saw the unfinished canvas accidentally left behind by those who had no idea we would come.

In Yarrow and in the other communities, I have seen very worthy manifestations of our goals. Here are some of them:

The farms at San Luis Rey Estates are the most beautiful I've had the joy to walk and work upon. This tract of sixty–two houses was only a small portion of the thousand stucco boxes intended for these rolling hills and wetlands of the seasonal river that winds down from Mount Palomar. A beautiful riparian jungle of reeds and low woodland must have been bulldozed away here, but over that irreparable wound the founders of this community planted a twenty–acre farm that is irrigated by the rising spring flows of that slowly recovering river, with only minimal use of the micro-drip hoses we have found so efficient.

Those crops requiring the most water and richest nutrients are planted closest to the wild flow, while the highest elevations of the gently graded banks are vividly dotted with the orange of pumpkins and yellow of squash, all topped with our vineyards and then the avocado trees and citrus. This small farm not only meets all the needs of our people there except for grains, but the surplus has been used to help feed the hungry throughout this rural part of the county as well as being sold or traded for needed supplies and equipment. That includes the windmill moved from an abandoned new mansion overlooking old Highway 395 — the community there traded a few crates of produce for the use of a semi-truck to haul the tower down to the farm. To stroll these rows at San Luis Rey Estates filled with our people happily working and children playing and the honeybees buzzing on the flowering plants is to be content on this Earth.

A man named Neal has coordinated the planting and harvesting there for a year or two now, and on my last visit he told me of a nightmare: He dreamed he was in his San Diego office park again, and the doors were locked from the outside. (Of course his San Diego office had no interest in keeping him; Neal was forced out a few months before his so–called retirement age, robbing him of most of his promised pension.)

At Goleta Fairways is the most beautiful common house I've seen. You know that this development was intended as a huge exclusive gated compound surrounding a full golf course. And one of the few nearly completed structures was this grand "clubhouse," which was also to serve as the sales office for this monstrous project over farms and wetlands at the foot of the Santa Rosa Hills, a solid hour's drive from the nearest small city. There were pretensions of modernist architecture in this building, best expressed in the walls of glass which would've overlooked eighteen holes of golf cart autopia, but look over the creek today and you see gardens and foot trails winding for miles around the community.

As in most of the structures in our communities, the floors are the bare concrete of the foundation just as they were left by the builders. But here they have been stained with a kind of hydrochloric acid solution that has reacted with the lime in the concrete to create a mottled reddish color. It is more beautiful than any ceramic tile I've seen, and can be easily cleaned with a bucket of water or a broom. The north wall of this long building is concrete block, which has been left in its original state, and the ceiling is made of exposed wood beams. It is unknown if a false ceiling was planned; in any case, it has been left the way it was found, open and airy.

That the building is little more than a rectangular shed with a wall of glass is mostly what gives it such serenity. There are rugs here and there on the floors and sections of the massive room holding bookshelves and chairs. As this is one of our most populous communities, there are nine simple wooden tables for the meals, arranged in a crescent around the woodstoves used for cooking and warmth. (There are also electric ovens left by the builders, which are attached to the solar panels on the roof.)

In the mornings and quiet afternoons you can find people sitting here and there, in meditation. Mealtimes are busy and there are all manner of activities and classes for children and adults throughout the day, from bread baking to violin lessons, yoga to oil painting. Later in the evening when most have gone to bed, you'll find a few gathered in conversation around what's left of the fire.

If it sounds like the idle life of a ski lodge or luxury resort, remember that everyone works in the gardens or maintaining the structures or whatever role they've chosen, and that the personal housing here is most austere, as only four of the massive homes were built enough to live in, and that upward of twenty people sleep in each of the separate houses. But even in these skeletal mansions, there is some privacy and comfort. One of these monstrosities has seven bedrooms! And the intended residents? From the looks of the faded developer's billboard on the narrow road leading to Goleta Fairways, two wealthy retired people would each have had one of these McMansions to themselves.

The community at Mojave Narrows has been most creative in transforming the ugly, unloved junk of the 2000s into a sanctuary for the heart. The only structures here were four clusters of strip mall, built for an intended exurban beehive of several thousand individual boxes, each with its "Spanish tile" roof and narrow, walled–off backyard of crushed rock over black plastic lining. The houses never arrived, although the virgin desert had been scraped by the earthmovers to make room for a handful of wood–frame skeletons. This wounded land was put to use for crops after the laborious cleaning of ragweed and other exotics that always rise in the wake of the bulldozer's destruction of the slow-growing native plants of that harsh environment.

Three of the four commercial clusters are low–rise L–shaped structures divided into stalls of about eighteen–hundred square feet apiece. These were to serve as the usual franchise locations of video–game rentals, pet supplies, lesser fast–food outlets, mortgage offices to sentence the working people to thirty years of monthly payments, and urgent care medical offices because the closest hospital was an hour away. A few brave local entrepreneurs would have leased the dregs for nail parlors and liquor stores, and the largest spot in each strip would have been reserved for an anchor tenant such as a drug store chain or medium–sized supermarket filled with freezer aisles of microwave meat suppers and corn–syrup cakes.

If this sounds dismal, you must remember the sites were also littered with construction debris and knocked–over portable toilets and the carpet of broken glass that appears whenever a structure is left alone for too long. But our founders here, the indefatigable Ursula and Ishiko, had a vision.

The biggest structure was a concrete–panel "big box" that would have housed an electronics and television store, or something of the kind. I almost wrote "Circuit City" but realized you would probably not remember that chain once seen at the crossroads of every exurban tract in America. This building was so charmless that the first people of this community naturally assumed it would be ignored, perhaps painted in colorful murals over time. What would one do with such an awful, unnatural thing?

The founders saw the triple gaping maw where the semi–trucks would have deposited the gadgets and gizmos from Asia, and computed the direction of the winds and the path of the sun through the seasons. The front of the building was utterly incomplete, with a fifty–foot–long hole missing the tall plastic and glass portico where the consumers would have entered. On the sides were a few human–sized doorways, minus the doors. It so happened that the morning sun kept the concrete hull filled with light until the heat of the Mojave midday, and the three vertical slots in the western wall provided a golden afternoon light that in summertime would last until the first stars appeared.

"The tender plants and flowers that would be scorched by direct desert sun, we'll put them along these east and west openings," Ishiko declared. "The center of the building will be our common house in the heat of the day, when all the other desert animals have the sense to go to their burrows."

And that is what they did with this unloved ruin. While the faceless architects of this monstrosity never intended to leave it open to the elements, by sheer dumb luck the grid they created was roughly aligned with both the sun's path and the usual movement of the wind — it is breezy, but the gusts that send sand and dust and Russian thistle tumbling across the land never quite get inside. In the center of the huge cube, when the days top a hundred degrees, it is possible to rest in comfort. Anyone who ever struggled to clear their busy mind for meditation has been assisted here by the cool concrete shelter during a broiling, sleepy afternoon.

As for the low–rise strips, these are the dormitories. They can be sweltering by day but always cool down at night. They are likewise chilly when the rare winter snows fall, but this is a relatively mild climate and anyone with a decent sleeping bag or wool blanket would sleep comfortably. So far, the small numbers of this community have left people more "personal space" than they probably ever had before the collapse. Each slot in the L–shaped strips could have accommodated fifty or sixty eaters or buyers, and now they are apartments shared by no more than ten denizens. The glass panel entrance walls were complete and intact in all but a couple of these cells, providing plenty of light and views of the surrounding desert.

Ursula followed the example set in the big box by placing the other crops in proximity to the three strips, so that all were protected in various measures from the extremes of the sun, saving much work in installing the kinds of cloth and plastic crop covers you've seen when fragile things are grown in the desert. In every way, they have put these existing structures to noble and beautiful uses.

This community at Mojave Narrows has been our model for so many new communities, because even where abandoned housing tracts are in short supply or have already been claimed by others, deserted strip malls can still be found.

Here I have told you of three very different examples, yet all adhere to B's instructions and to the spirit of Yarrow. As you prepare to lead others in the founding of new communities, keep these images in your mind — and keep your mind open to entirely new ways of looking at that which has been discarded by the old system.

Remember what B said when he was challenged about the use of these vulgar developments, and the people asked why it wasn't better to build new things of "sustainable materials" and all that: "The house that hurts the Earth the least is the house that's already there."

N

8

To my dear friends at Mojave Narrows,

The terrible news has reached me here, and I grieve with you all.

I hope everyone made it safely away before the attack. It pains me to think of your beautiful gardens and apartments destroyed by these cold souls.

Salvatore must have done everything in his power to stop this in the courts, but the courts are not on our side.

I will keep this short and pass it on with Francesca who will rendezvous with you up north.

My mind is empty of wisdom or encouraging words, except for these that B told us before he was taken away:

"In their sickness, they will strike out at those in good health."

N

9

To my dear friends at Cabernet Ridge,

It may help to know more about what was unraveling around us when the shop was in existence. Los Angeles has always had its share of riots and unrest, being a patchwork of poor districts and ethnic enclaves and working–class districts in the flatlands, with the rich areas looking down on them from the foothills. This has been the case ever since the sleepy pueblo of the *Californios* began to be subdivided and sold in single–family bits, back in the 1880s.

Combined with the world crisis and the retreat of both the federal and state operations that sustained so many, the leaders of this sprawling metropolis chopped away at those things most needed — buses for workers without cars, medical clinics for the poor, rent assistance, even the air–conditioned cooling stations that helped so many of the old and the ill survive the scorching heat waves that stretched over ever longer summers. The few banks and grocery stores that served these weary neighborhoods began to close down or move away, and countless families were locked out of their humble houses through foreclosure. Abandoned dogs roamed the wide cracked streets of dead lawns and auction signs and uncollected garbage, the hungry housecats hiding in the shadows from coyotes and hawks. Those who had lived through the Watts uprising and Rodney King riots told me it was as if the art of urban devastation had finally been perfected — this time, there were no flames, no columns of toxic smoke with police helicopters circling overhead and sirens wailing. This time, the siege was quiet and computerized.

Of course it was happening everywhere except inside the richest enclaves, but in the suburbs it was difficult to see the scale. One block might be left untouched and the next, hidden within a cul–de–sac, might be completely vacant with nothing but those rectangles of white paper in the front windows to tell of what happened.

What we had in our Echo Park neighborhood, after a decade of uneasy truce between the longtime immigrant population and the newcomers who sought out the area's cheaper rents, was complete disruption and upheaval. In the final years before the crash, the developers had followed the trail of coffeehouses and ethnic restaurants and found a place to build elaborate new apartment towers and luxury condominiums that neither of the existing populations could hope to afford. But few of these obscene projects were completed before the crisis, and many residents had been uprooted just as a wave of job loss and foreclosure washed over town and the basic services that had helped people survive began to disappear. The crime and despair returned almost overnight, and the stressed police forces from the infamous Rampart division station responded in the usual way: more shootings, more brutality, more abuse as the paranoid circle of fear and despair created even more violence and horror.

Our meals continued. And through the power brownouts and endless sirens and screams of anguish heard through the open windows of Vera and Tommy's bungalow balanced on that eroding cliff, our meals became more somber, more ritualized. Even then, B would try to steer us away from sorrow, asking, "Is the food spoiled? Is the wine bad?" And we would regain our determination.

Tommy lost his work first, but he was hardly the last. Within a single grim week, four of our little group had been cut off from their income. This is how we began the practice of saying to one another at the blessing of the meal, "My work is here with you" — because the work we had known was slipping away, and we had to learn how to live without these structures.

There were eleven of us, then, and we invented the habit of choosing four to do the cooking and serving and cleaning for the others, because it was impossible to fit more than four people into Vera and Tommy's narrow kitchen. So one evening it would be, for example, Celia and Tobias and Ursula and B. And then onward to the next four, and the next, even if the math never quite worked out. It was not a chore to cook and serve, it was a pleasure. And ever since, whenever we sit to celebrate the meal, four take care of that table and the others are free to engage their minds and senses for the equally important task of offering conversation and eating the food with thoughtfulness.

It was at such a dinner that the shop began to take shape. Not one of us sitting there thought it was especially important to the work we were beginning — it was just a simple way for Tommy to clear out this unwanted stuff in a way that would help our neighbors. A few of us were in the garden every day, and this way whoever was around could help give away Tommy's surplus.

So we swept out the concrete lot and hauled all the boxes and bins around the block and lined everything along the walls of the buildings opposite — a vacant coin laundry and the back of a discount car parts store. While sorting through the things he didn't need, Tommy found a Happy Birthday banner from some forgotten party and used the blank side to write "0¢ Store" with a black marker, in mock tribute to the 99–cent store up on Sunset. With this declaration hanging over the used goods, the shop was open for non–business. We expected people to simply stop by and sort through the stuff and take what they wanted, which some people did. But others — especially those in the neighborhood who were now sharing the garden — started bringing their own unneeded things.

The zero–cent store turned out to be exactly what a lot of people needed as that harsh summer finally gave way to an imperceptible autumn. Money had never been so tight, not in any of our lives, while the insanity of the real estate collapse was broadsiding even families and singles who had no mortgage at all. The old white three–story apartment building on the corner of Portia Street had been seized by a lender and then sold at auction, and the next week the police came to push out the renters, mostly immigrant families, so that rents could be doubled. The police were sent for this! (The building was still vacant when I last saw Echo Park.)

So people were moving in with relatives or slogging back to Central America or going to the overburdened homeless shelters or living in shame in the backseats of their beat–up cars. And they suddenly had so many things they didn't need or couldn't carry. We all had so much stuff. I would marvel at the piles of televisions and cribs and toys and kitchen gadgets that came out of the humblest one–bedroom apartments. Never before had poor people had so much of the wrong things.

We argued thoughtfully and sometimes not so thoughtfully about our complicity, if that's the word, in shuffling these chunks of plastic and electronics from one person to another. Should it not all be dismantled and used to make noble things? In theory, but who would see that through? Was someone going to stow away inside a shipping container of disassembled gadgets headed back to China and then direct the factories to make wheelbarrows from the reclaimed plastic, or medical devices from discarded video games?

And so we compromised, as everyone must do unless they plan to take on the whole world alone. Whatever a person needed, we gave it freely — but we made sure they also left with a sack of fresh greens from the garden.

A woman from Tobias' office came by with sample packages of baby supplies — infant diapers, that kind of thing — that the hospital downtown provided to expectant mothers. She had given birth the summer before and had never opened this care package until her child was too big to use any of it. No sooner had she set the package down that a young mother grabbed it up. Jane mentioned that all her friends who gave birth at that hospital had the same unused blue packages, and maybe we should post something online to solicit these valuable little parcels.

B popped up from the back of the lot, where he was assembling a tricycle dropped off in pieces, and stared at us with curiosity.

I don't recall who actually did it, but the notices went up on the listings websites and the so–called social networks. And very soon there were a lot more people coming around, both to drop off things and to volunteer their time. Some were colleagues, comrades, acquaintances at least. Others were new to us, and a few struck me as too intense for such a friendly neighborhood pursuit. If anything demands quiet contemplation and group discourse, it's the acceptance of strangers into your community. But we just let it happen.

B left us for some time, as was his habit. When he returned, we proudly told him of the progress — there were now three shops, or non–shops, and we had started a new garden across the I–5 in Highland Park. For all this, we owed a lot to one of those passionate newcomers, who called himself "Gary Green." Gary was his real name, he said, while "Green" he claimed was earned by his volunteer work with so many good causes. He was full of ideas. B was polite but guarded, as we all should have been. Celia immediately dubbed him "Gary Greener Than Thou."

There never should've been a shop on Glendale Boulevard. It was a busy street and we were calling attention to what had been a quiet neighborhood effort. Worse, we shouldn't have been soliciting donations in the way we began to, online. But Gary had ingratiated himself and then appointed himself the host of the Glendale vacant lot. And then one evening at a meal that was tense and unhappy, he mumbled something to B about a delivery of infant formula and baby clothes that "fell off a truck."

B stood up, glaring through the candlelight at Gary sitting at the end of the table with his muscular arms crossed in front of him.

"Come with me," B said to Salvatore. "The rest of you stay here, with him."

"Hey come on," Gary said, shrugging.

The police were waiting at the lot. They arrested B and charged him with larceny and grand theft and a few other felonies.

Salvatore would have been taken downtown, too, but he was driving around the block looking for a legal place to park. When he saw the officers pushing B into the back of the squad car, he just followed it down to the jail and went inside after a while to identify himself as B's counsel. This mystified them as B had yet to make his phone call.

N

10

To the Cabernet Ridge community,

My apologies for sending the last letter unfinished.
Susanna arrived unexpectedly and it is a good thing she
did, because our tormentors had figured out I was at
_____ and she was able to assist my escape before the
raid. I have since learned the community was needlessly
harassed for many days, but no–one was arrested or
harmed as there was no evidence the people knew
anything of B.

The years pass, and their tactics are just as clumsy and
cruel and stupid. We can only hope that more of them
see the injustice of what they do and one day refuse to
persecute us.

I told you of B's arrest on Glendale Boulevard, after
an infiltrator had so easily shown us to be fools. The
district attorney insisted on a trial, with all the hysterical
local media coverage he could generate during that

autumn of unhappiness. They attempted to portray B as some kind of degenerate Robin Hood who stole from small shopkeepers and then gave the stuff away to unsavory people who were no better than thieves themselves. An "economic predator targeting our weakest neighborhoods," that was one of the florid charges thrown at B in the county courthouse and duly repeated by the television news that night.

Until that farce of justice, it had never occurred to us that simply growing vegetables and helping our neighbors could be seen as a threat to anyone. B did not welcome the infiltrator or encourage the publicity of our efforts, but he didn't speak against it. We should have paid more attention. Instead, our heads were growing with pride because we were doing something meaningful for once.

While we waited for B's trial, we got well acquainted with the full bureaucratic brunt of the city and state. Health inspectors, safety inspectors, code enforcement officers and the collectors from the Franchise Tax Board began a full–time campaign of annoyance and harassment. And just when we would seem to shake one away, more would show up from other divisions or entirely different departments. The California tax agents were especially dogged because they refused to believe we had no financial records, no bank account, no evidence of transacting money at all. Salvatore would start talking about "barter" and "charity" and they'd drop another pile of regulations on us — why weren't we registered as a nonprofit, then? Why weren't we paying the "use tax"?

Then the taxmen and code officers began calling our homes and our work numbers — those of us who still had workplaces, anyway — and ominous document packages from the state and county and federal governments began showing up in our mailboxes. The authorities and bureaucracies suddenly had our names and they knew where we went during the day — they even started harassing friends and acquaintances who had never set foot on the lots, who had no involvement whatsoever. Jane took me aside and asked if I remembered her roommate who had moved to Oregon months before we planted the first garden.

"The FBI showed up at her house in Eugene, asking about B," Jane said. "What kind of foolish trap have we set for ourselves?"

The trap was set on our screens. Everyone we knew being harassed by the police and tax collectors and code cops had made their innocent support of our neighborhood project known, just by joining its "social networks." Some were actually involved, others had just clicked "add" or "like" because their friends and acquaintances online had done the same. It was all there for anyone to see, as long as they were our "friend."

Gary Greener Than Thou had been quick to hit us all up online, to be his virtual buddies. And once welcomed to our online lives, he and anyone else with the interest could see where we were, what we were doing, what causes we supported, what farmers markets we frequented, and of course when the zero-cent shops and our community gardens were open for non–business.

Jane and I looked at the screen together in horror. Gary had let all kinds of other militants into our mundane little corner of the social network, and they had filled the comments and message sections with calls to rise up and topple the industrial food industry and boycott the banks and block Highway 101 through downtown with burning garbage.

When the Internal Revenue Service people showed up in person, they were fuming because there was no structure to our "entity." Salvatore or Jane or Tobias would explain we had simply started a couple of neighborhood gardens in vacant lots and made use of a few spots on the street where people could exchange unwanted things. (The third shop up the street had been abandoned without discussion after B was arrested there and "Gary Green" vanished forever, only to reappear at B's trial as a witness for the prosecution.)

What maddened us was the sheer number of officers and agents descending on our neighborhood while broken stoplights blinked incessantly and bus stops were untroubled by buses and the elementary school was locked up and fenced off for lack of staff and budget. And then one afternoon as I sat guard at the garden, with the old men next door now rude and snarling toward us because they too had been harassed by all manner of officialdom, a man I knew walked up to our little plot. He carried a clipboard and wore a computer–phone on his belt along with the dull uniform of a city bureaucrat — short–sleeved shirt, necktie, pants just one step up from jeans. We had worked on a nonprofit project together years earlier on the Los Angeles River, getting the deeds to unwanted little scraps of land near the concrete channel for use as "pocket parks." He didn't recognize me for a moment, and then gave a brief smile of acknowledgement before accusing me of five or six municipal code violations.

"This is crazy," I told him. "We have a community garden. There are community gardens all over. Aren't you supposed to be helping create these kinds of spaces?"

He motioned for me to walk, so I walked with him to the end of our garden lot, our backs now facing the street. Were these rows of lettuce and squash now under surveillance, too?

"My whole department's gone," he said. "There's no money to think about pocket parks. I don't know what you guys are doing here but the whole city's going nuts about it."

I told him we weren't doing anything that wasn't perfectly visible to anyone who bothered to look, and that the whole false controversy was the work of some failed *agent provocateur* from the LAPD who thought we were giving away stolen goods.

"That's not my problem," he said. "I'm down to three days of paid work a week, but they act like I'm getting overtime. Everybody's on forced furloughs but the supervisors. You guys rubbed somebody wrong enough that the DA has at least two people doing nothing but trying to find the owners of these parcels so you can all be arrested for felony criminal trespass."

(I write this from memory; there may have been other crimes he mentioned, or this one may have had a slightly different name. I do remember "felony" very well.)

I actually laughed at the trespassing threat. Salvatore had spent weeks trying to track down human owners of these lots and had hit one dead end after another — we very much wanted permission to use the parcels. Like so much real estate, these properties had fallen into default and receivership and then a weird limbo because the mortgage holders were not actual people or even institutions. Each mortgage had been carved by computer into little shreds of loan risk and collateral that were bundled and unbundled and divided like cells and repackaged and resold through a hundred different channels, most of which had themselves collapsed or been subsumed by this or that agency or trust or government. Nobody could find the owners, not just of these sorry little cracked concrete lots but for millions of failed real estate deals all over the state and the whole country!

My former colleague didn't share my amusement. He warned me to get away from the whole neighborhood. "Somebody is completely spooked by what you're doing here, and they think it's a lot more than gardens and garage–sale junk."

When I asked what else could possibly be involved, he just shrugged and walked away. At about two or three the next morning, marshals and city maintenance crews in bulldozers showed up and razed our half–acre garden, smashed and hauled away everything in the shop lot, then headed to Highland Park to finish off the garden there. In the process of scraping away our original garden, an earthmover nicked the retaining wall under the old guys' cottage. It collapsed a few days later, the thin 1920s walls and tarpaper and cheap broken windows and splintery little two–by–four studs in a sad pile atop their murdered avocado and lemon trees. The city crews felt no need to clean any of this mess up, and our poor old neighbors moved to a boardinghouse down past Korea Town while their insurance company refused to pay a dollar.

As for B, his bail was refused because the prosecution said he was a flight risk — he had no fixed address and lived in shabby old German diesel van that ran on used cooking grease he either picked up at a clandestine dispensary in East Hollywood or requested from the service doors of roadside restaurants on his travels. No matter that he had grown up in Southern California and had never been away for more than a few months in his life. We took turns visiting him in jail downtown, and while it always seemed to cheer him up, whoever went that week always came back depressed.

It was midway through that drab L.A. winter when his trial finally began. It mostly consisted of the district attorney's people reading from online comments or showing surveillance photographs of B cleaning up the lots and pulling weeds in the garden. Gary Greener Than Thou put on a typically intense and melodramatic performance, his eyes darting around wildly and the muscles in his neck twitching as he claimed B had planned a complete disruption of commercial activity on the East Side of Los Angeles, and that these actions were just the beginning. Sometimes I was so incensed by these bogus claims that I had to leave the courtroom and sit outside until I could regain my breathing and composure, but B just sat there with a relaxed expression, alert but unworried.

The only verdict the jury could agree on was something about harboring stolen goods at the Glendale Boulevard lot where the infiltrator had admittedly placed the stolen goods. For this non–crime, B was sentenced to six months in county jail along with an hour or two of insults and threats from the judge. As for the rest of us watching from the back of the courtroom, we had been warned against "making a scene" and threatened with arrest if anyone so much as shed a tear at sentencing.

So we sat there, stone–faced and saddened, as the bailiffs led B away and he glanced back to give us a half–smile.

N

11

To the community at Quail Meadows Ridge,

Your letter reached me at Adobe Terrace, and I am happy to have the drawings from the children. Actual quail at Quail Meadows Ridge! This would surely surprise the tract's builders, after they worked so diligently to bulldoze every trace of nature from the land you now call home.

Be cheerful, and do not let the bad news darken the life you are building there in the desert. From a derelict idol to greed and defilement, you are making a humane village and a peaceful refuge from the world that spit you out. When the wild creatures are walking among you again, as they are beginning to do now, you know the land has welcomed you to these wounded acres.

Now I will deal with the problems you are making for yourselves. Hatred of another's skin color or whether they love their own gender, these attitudes are inexcusable in our communities. Do not "hold meetings" or any such thing. The person or persons claiming to be offended by such things will be removed from the community. Give them one opportunity to renounce their hatreds and beg forgiveness from the fellowship — and if this fails to happen, sincerely, then send them out at once.

It worries me that you report these kinds of mean and petty disputes. Do you let anyone into your community? Yes, everyone is welcome, if there is space and enough food to go around, but this is only if they vow to live as we do: in harmony with the others in the community, in harmony with the natural world around us and, most important, at peace with themselves.

We all suffer stresses and we all endured much before we found our homes, and nobody should be turned away for being wounded in the ceaseless battle that came to define our pointless "lifestyle" before the crises. But those who are incapable of living in peace within our community are a toxin to all of us. If B himself could not survive the infiltration of traitors, do you think you can?

How good it will be when all of humanity can be part of our community. But that will not be accomplished by poisoning ourselves with those who are not ready to join us. Send them out. And do *not* ask me how to go about it — I am not a policeman and I will not invent the hard solutions for you.

We face real dangers and more of our communities are under real, outside attack. Do not complain to me about people you've allowed to come inside and share your meals at the table. The community is your home, and you alone are responsible for keeping it free of vermin.

N

12

To the brothers and sisters at Ocotillo Ranchos,

I hope things are going well for your new community, and it is my intention to visit you there once it is safe for me to leave Elora again. Thank you for the detailed list of the crops coming up and the houses you have rehabilitated. I wish I could advise of a way to deal with your water issues. From the rows of plastic tubing and the little meters you've installed, you're getting as much from that trickle of water as anyone could expect. Is a well even a possibility there? If so, barter with the well driller — we know he can't have much paying work anymore, so a year's worth of weekly vegetable baskets might make a real difference not only to your water supply but to the wellness of this man and his family.

On the question of screens, and why they are prohibited in our communities, I would rather not write some detailed argument. Are there exceptions to this prohibition? Yes, but they aren't codified and they shouldn't be codified.

You know it is good to work and exercise in the sunshine and fresh air, and that you become slow and sickly if you fall out of the healthful routine. It isn't necessary to have a list of regulations explaining why this is so — you *know* it to be true, you feel it physically and mentally.

Likewise, you know that you gave so much of your previous life to the screens, staring into that gaping void from a soft couch or a padded office chair or even while eating with your friends and family. You know your insatiable appetite for amusement and titillation and banal exchanges with disembodied "friends" made you physically weak and mentally stunted. Let that be all the reason you need to keep your community free of this poison.

It is true that a growing distaste for the habit of staring into a screen all the time became a total denunciation after B's trial and imprisonment in Los Angeles, and after our young community was nearly destroyed by officialdom convinced we had sinister motives — all of this was fueled by the screens, by the groups and likes and messages and comments. We had exposed ourselves terribly, and allowed infiltrators to enter these empty virtual worlds at our invitation! Had we kept our garden in the genuine world, those undercover troublemakers would still be ignorant of our existence!

And once we were forced to separate and run, how easy was it for our persecutors to find those of us carrying the little screens in our purses and pockets. We were broadcasting our exact location to them. We were fools, and the price we paid was severe.

It was many years later, when I shared the meal with a new community at Descanso Hills, that I learned just how tangled our neighborhood efforts had become in the wider movements just beginning to happen at that time, mostly without our knowledge. We had been liked, linked, favorited, forwarded and friended through a web of supposedly similarly minded people and groups. And several of these virtual do–gooders were simple fronts for the intelligence services, tax collectors, state and local police, even the federal food safety agency — the USDA was chasing after backyard gardeners and co–op dairies rather than worry about the industrial toxins fed into our bodies and our Earth by the petrochemical corn and slaughter industry.

The exact link that brought the bureaucratic rage of the officials down upon us was something called Opt Out of America. I had never heard the name then, but it was a fiery group pledging to accelerate the collapse of our troubled country by its members' refusal to buy unnecessary things and to take trains or aircraft as long as the Transportation Security forces continued harassing and humiliating paying passengers. Like our own small group, they also vowed to grow as much of their own food as possible, and in general avoid participation in the poisonous culture.

Opt Out of America was, of course, a cheap and easy way for the government to collect information on the millions of people who sympathized with these peaceful methods of change. But the Los Angeles authorities didn't know this, and they closely watched the invented movement's online activity in Southern California. When our little group was noticed by the larger, make–believe group, the LAPD put us on the domestic enemies list, which in turn alerted the federal authorities to our existence. Only then did the harassment begin in earnest. It would all be comical if the consequences hadn't been so horrific.

You say you are untroubled by police or authorities today, that even the local deputies have stopped by to pick up vegetables and flowers for their families. That is good and I hope it continues. But if you paint a wireless bulls–eye on your community, the arrow will find its way to you.

N

13

To the community at San Luis Rey Estates,

How is the work at your little village there by the river? I hope the well is still keeping the gardens green and that you are not troubled by the police and bankers.

Your letter took a long time to reach me, as I've had to do plenty of traveling myself. Melinda crossed my path at Tejon Ranch with a packet of letters collected from all around California. The questions from your group at San Luis Rey have brought many memories to mind.

As to our habit of stargazing on Winter Solstice, it began by chance. Or what seemed like chance to the eight of us with B on that desert voyage. Perhaps B had planned it all along.

Some of us had expected to stay at Yarrow, but B put an end to that idea once he was turned loose by the Los Angeles County jailers for the second time. The cause of this second arrest was more absurd than the first: While hiking the wash in hopes of spotting the mountain lion again, B instead came across a couple of drunken louts spinning circles through the wildflowers in their four-wheel-drive pickup. He asked them to please go somewhere else. The older man instead pulled a gun and identified himself as an off-duty San Bernardino County deputy sheriff. B was arrested for "making terroristic threats." B's parole in L.A. County turned up on the sheriff's department computer system.

We remained ignorant of all this until Javier pulled up in his taxi some days later, explaining that B was in jail. Javier was the only one at Yarrow who had a phone, so that was the number B had dialed for his one call. Salvatore rode back to Los Angeles with Javier the next morning but failed to get B out.

It was a December evening when B finally returned to Yarrow, pedaling an old "beach cruiser" bicycle he picked up somewhere in the city and rode over the mountains. The girls saw him coming up the road and they ran from house to house, yelling that B had come home.

After the meal that night, which we had in the common house with everyone crowded around our long table, B said nothing of his latest imprisonment and instead told us it was time to move onward. There were gasps, and at once Javier's wife began to babble and cry, with Javier himself standing stoically, the little girls tugging at him and laughing over some game they'd made up. Then B said that of course Javier's family should stay at Yarrow, and that other families would soon be part of the community, too.

B then spoke to the eight of us, saying, "Tomorrow you will go into Victorville and then Palmdale. Find people in need who will be happy at Yarrow. Four houses will be open once we leave."

"How do we just find people who would want to live out here?" asked Nicholas. "Who would take care of gardens and walk around the desert?"

B scowled at him and said, "Didn't you once spend your days writing computer software that could find anything? Can't you figure out where the food banks and social services are, and use your eyes to see good families in need?"

"Well sure," Nicholas said, looking at his plate. "Just tell me what you want me to do, is all I'm saying."

"I am not here to tell you what to do," B said. "You either know what to do or you joined this community by mistake."

The next afternoon, Nicholas introduced us to three families subsisting off food donations and sharing crowded homes with many others on the most desperate edges of town. The families were a mix of single mothers and small children and grandmothers and one father who had lost his construction job some time ago and was raising boys of ten and twelve years old. The remaining three houses were filled with the newcomers' friends and a few more strangers, all gentle people who were trying to keep afloat in an endless flood.

With the new arrivals came a beat–up Ford minivan with a month remaining on its registration, and at the meal that night B said it would take us where we were going next. Of the nine, B said Nicholas and Ursula would remain, and that Celia would drive the van on the journey.

"When we arrived here two seasons ago," B said to her, "you accused me of wanting to drive you away. Now you will drive *me* away, but you will return to Yarrow."

Celia laughed and shook her head and said, "I never thought I would love this place."

"You can love any place once *you* show it love," B answered. "Now let's make sure our new friends feel at home."

With that, B disappeared into the kitchen and returned with pies he'd been baking that afternoon, all filled with the fresh berries we grew right outside the houses. The slices he cut fell apart on the plates, but one of the new children said, "It's better than a McDonald's apple pie," and Celia muttered that she sure hoped it was better than that.

We loaded our backpacks and sleeping bags and a big plastic ice chest full of fruit and vegetables and tamales that Javier's wife had made for the holidays. Everything happened so quickly that none of us had time to grieve for our Yarrow, our Yarrow we had built from a handful of abandoned half–constructed tract houses.

Looking over the thick gardens and green–roofed houses surrounded by flowers and sunlight, with kids playing between the farmed yards and adults talking happily as they pulled weeds and picked tomatoes, I felt a sudden stab of loss and did not want to leave. In the city I had labored to create places where families could live meaningful lives with dignity and fresh food and what little bit of nature we could corral inside an apartment courtyard or vacant lot. And here, in this unfinished housing tract abandoned by the world of bankers, we had built a true oasis without compromise.

For the working men and toiling women who had been told there was no longer a place for them at the table, we had built a table of plenty that was long enough for all who arrived.

B approached me as I gazed back on our community.

"It's a good thing you've done here, but don't be too proud," B said. "Wait until you've built another hundred Yarrows."

Celia drove up the I–15 for an hour or two and looked over at B. He just nodded at the windshield and she kept driving up through the Mojave. At Baker we stopped for gas and water and saw a road sign that said "Death Valley National Park."

"That's where we will spend the solstice," B said.

The narrow road wound around the scorched mountains and dipped in and out of dry desert washes. At the junction we stopped to stretch our legs and shivered in the cold blasting wind. Purple clouds hung over the peaks of the distant Panamint Range, a winter storm trying to leap over that vertical line of pine–topped mountains before they squeezed all the moisture out.

The old van creaked and rocked as Celia drove it over the low pass and into Death Valley itself. Rain and sleet pelted the windshield. The campground at Furnace Creek had a wooden "FULL" sign blocking the driveway, but a line of campers and cars were coming out and a park ranger in a Smokey Bear hat and thin windbreaker stepped out of the booth to lower the chain and let us through.

She squinted through the snow flurries and said, "Reservations?"

"None," said B, leaning over Celia. "Just here for the night."

"Everybody's leaving anyway," the ranger said. "Nobody wants to camp in this. Take anything open, they're all paid for already."

B thanked her and we found a campsite that was sheltered by two big tamarisk trees, invasive species that made excellent desert windbreaks while sucking the water table dry. We had one dome tent that might hold four people. The rest would have to sleep in the van or freeze outside. By now the snow was sticking to the split–rail fence along the campground's loop.

We ate tamales and berries, huddling around the picnic table as the cold wind lashed us around and sent corn husks flying.

"You're all true pioneers," B said through a shiver. "And I'm ready to sit by a fireplace."

The Furnace Creek restaurant was open but not very crowded. All the tent campers had fled, and the only diners were older people staying in RVs or the motel there. The waitress said we looked like frozen rats and led us to a group table by the woodstove. Everyone ordered coffee or hot tea, and some asked for soup and warm bread and B requested a bottle of red wine.

I had not set foot in a restaurant for six or eight months. The waitress was kind and said she lived on the little Indian reservation that was right there alongside the national park offices and campgrounds and the little grocery store.

Celia poured the wine and passed the glasses around the table.

"There is always something to celebrate," B said. "Twice a year we have a solstice, twice a year we have an equinox. Celebrate these — everybody else does! The New Year, Easter, summer, harvest."

We ate and drank and warmed ourselves in the cozy, empty restaurant.

"I feel like we need to *learn* more," Jane said after we finished. "Like someone—" she looked at B "—should be *telling* us more."

B paid the waitress with the roll of money he occasionally produced from his pocket, and he smiled at each of us sitting at the table around him.

"Follow me," he said.

Outside it was still very cold, but the storm clouds had blown over and the air was clean and clear. We walked through the big campground, following B, who suddenly turned away from our site and went directly to a long silver–colored camper trailer attached to a green pickup truck. On the other side of the trailer, shielded from the worst of the wind and the light from the camp buildings, was a man in a fur–collared parka working at a huge telescope. This man also wore a park ranger hat, although he didn't wear the uniform.

"Ranger," B said, "do you know a lot about the stars?"

"Can always learn more," the man said with a grin. "I'm an astronomy professor up at Flagstaff. We do winter stargazing programs here for the holidays but I guess nobody's up for camping in a blizzard. See that?"

We looked to the east where he pointed, to a dim glow over the mountains.

"That's the light from Las Vegas and its suburbs. They just crept up and crept up and I thought they'd never stop crawling toward the wilderness — until they stopped. Without dark skies, you can't see a damned thing. When that big quake hit Northridge in the nineties and knocked all the power out, people ran outside and were amazed to see stars everywhere, even the Milky Way like you see so clear here, a big fat ribbon of stars right over Los Angeles."

B smiled and said, "Can we look at the stars with you?"

We then spent a pleasant hour taking turns at the telescope, looking at Jupiter and its moons — which the astronomer said was especially close to Earth this year — and at many clusters of galaxies and distant stars.

"People quit paying attention to the stars when we all went inside at night to watch TV," the astronomer said. "But one day we'll want to know about them again."

Celia asked, "Why's that?"

"Because we'll be out there, someday. And those of us back here on the good old Earth will stand outside at night and say, 'That's where Joey went,' or 'Sally's headed toward Perseus now.' Or maybe we *won't* ever go. And in that case, we'll probably start dying out here on good old Earth in the next hundred thousand years or so. We'll need the stars again then, too."

"Thank you for the program," B said. "Happy Solstice to you."

We walked back to our campsite in silence, and as B spread his sleeping bag on the soft sand under the cold night sky, he said to all of us, "And now you've learned more."

N

14

To the new community at Antelope Canyon,

You are strangers to me today, but I hope to meet you in person soon and share in the fellowship of your new village. As for the efforts you've made so far, they are inspiring to read about — you may be the very first of our communities to rise from an existing neighborhood! That so many of your neighbors have joined in completely and that so few have moved away is the greatest testimony to the wisdom of our ways that I can imagine.

Of course every community is different, but your experiment is unique. That you would seek to have a book of rules to govern and guide you is only logical. And I'm sure I will disappoint with my answer: We have no codified guide of conduct. That is for each community to figure out on its own, because the very act of being alive is a compromise made between our environment and ourselves and our fellow humans.

What I can give you is one example of how a community might form and prosper. Yarrow was created from the ruins of our uninitiated life in Echo Park. What grew out of parched desert and abandoned tract there in the Mojave was an improvisation that very rapidly settled into a strict routine we welcomed because *our lives had fallen apart.*

It is easy to look back, from this distance of space and time, and say that we so plainly needed a way to replace the methods and habits of our past with something pure and new. We embraced the new methods as fast as we could invent them. Writing those words, they strike me as vain — we invented nothing, really. As B said, "Once you stop running and open your eyes, everything is perfectly simple and obvious."

And so it was obvious that we did not need to deliberate over much. The sun is our clock and our calendar and our creator. We rise with it, we celebrate the meal when it sets, we plant according to its movements, and we mark our seasons by its stations in the sky.

First Light — A walk in nature, contemplation of the dawn.

Sunrise — A communal breakfast.

Morning — Work on the farm and the village.

Midday — A light meal taken outside or in small groups, followed by rest or contemplation.

Afternoon — Work on the farm and the village followed by time for study, art, reflection, exercise, music.

Sundown — The celebration of the evening meal, followed by fellowship.

Night — Contemplation and sleep.

We all loved bells, and so we used bells as so many communities have done since the dawn of metallurgy. But at Yarrow we had no bells, so Salvatore took to striking the seven passages on the copper cooking pots that hung in the common house kitchen. There was a music in the way the wooden spoon would clang against that well–used cookware. And we all liked it very much.

On festival days we did not work, other than those on kitchen duty. (We attempted to rotate these solstice and equinox shifts, just as we took turns serving and cleaning for our daily meals.) After some time we set aside Saturday for the doing of nothing in particular, but often changed it to Tuesday because that was the day Javier had off work from the taxicab company and could spend at Yarrow with his wife and children. And then it changed back to Saturday again, once Javier lost his job and quit trying to pay off the many debts accumulated by his little daughters for the sins of being born poisoned and uninsured.

On full moon nights, we let the children stay up late and play in the lunar light — the adults enjoyed it just as much, spraying each other with snowballs in the wintertime or walking the cool and eerie landscape after the heat of a summer day.

It never felt to me like we had sacrificed anything. Commuter traffic? Television? The lost–forever hours staring into the void of the screen, clicking this or that, feeling empty and tired?

We had, in Echo Park, already divorced ourselves from many pathologies. So the creation of Yarrow was eased much by all that we had put aside in the crumbling city.

But, compared to almost all the communities that have risen since, Yarrow was the most disciplined, the most devoted. In our year together there, which raced by so quickly and mainly so contentedly, many questions never arose. We had good health, our surplus from the gardens was easily sold or traded for whatever we lacked, and the exuberance of figuring stuff out was enough to lift the community over the inevitable ditches and disappointments that are as much a part of a good life as the happiness. And we were fierce in the prohibition of screens, phones, tablets, whatever you want to call them, whatever they are called now.

The fullness of the poison of the screen had revealed itself only during the attack on our Echo Park community. We were utterly unprepared for policemen and tax collectors hiding behind friendly names on the screen. We never expected a neighborhood vegetable garden to attract such petty, official evil. We had all grown used to these machines in our pockets and purses, these screens watching us from tables and desks at work and at home, and we were naïve.

And when I say "we" what I really mean is "all of us, except for B." He had known for years. He lived free from the jaws of cell phone contracts and pop-up advertisements and social pornography and the beeping, whirring, twittering inanity of industrially caged hens proclaiming their digital freedom of expression even as the cold wire of the pens slowly sawed through their thin bones. He, unlike the rest of us, *did not exist on the Internet.*

Not that it helped B, his precognition in these matters. He sank under the weight of our thoughtless addictions.

Anyway, you seek instruction and not my conflicted recollections of a time that recedes deeper into the past of our strange century.

Let me end with this: There is *no perfect way*, no single list or rule book that will serve in all situations. And, because your last letter made so many references to "old ways" known only to us from history, I will remind you that there was no perfect *past*, either. You drop the names of empires and eras without a word about the injustice of those times. Would you wear a laurel and have slaves serve your meals? Would you keep women silent at your table?

We are the makers of this new map of the world. Our time is the culmination of everything — good and bad, just and unjust — that came before us. But our direction comes from our own navigation.

N

15

To the community at San Luis Rey Estates,

This is the second part of my letter to your village. I hope it finds you all well, and I hope you have some memory of the first part!

Now let me tell you about that day, the shortest of the year, when we were forced to learn much more. The white sun rose over the mountains and flooded the campground with that intense winter light you get on a clear desert morning after a storm.

Water was boiling on the camp stove when I stepped out of the old van, full of stale air from three people sleeping all night on its bench seats. The tent was unoccupied, its flap door unzipped. I thought for a moment I'd been left behind when I saw them all walking back from a morning hike.

"You slept through the solstice dawn," Celia called out to me. "Is B back?"

I saw then he wasn't with them and I said no, I had not seen B.

As the five of them sat around the stove to make tea, I looked at the depression in the sand where B had slept. I poked my head inside the tent, but his backpack and sleeping bag were not inside. Finally I opened the cargo doors of the van.

"B took his things," I said.

They all spun around and stared at me. All except Celia, who sipped her tea and stared out to the west. We then split up, all except Celia, to the ranger booth and visitor center and restaurant. It was Tobias who spoke to the young ranger who had let us take the campsite the night before.

The ranger had seen B walking out of the campground with his pack, about a half–hour before sunrise, as she was driving to work from the national park's village up the road. B said he intended to hike up Telescope Peak, and she said it would be a hard climb with the new snow. He laughed and went to the highway, where she saw him stick out his thumb and then catch a ride in a pickup coming out of the Timbisha reservation. The trailhead was about an hour up the road at Mahogany Flat.

We argued about what to do and soon T was yelling and I was yelling back.

I asked, "Can we not even make a decision if B's not here?"

Celia said we could, and that we should just go to the trailhead and wait for B to come down. After all, it was thirty degrees colder up there, eleven thousand feet above the dry valley. I worried if he had an ice axe in his pack or anything of the sort.

We ate without enthusiasm and made use of the showers at the campground and finally loaded up the van and were ready to drive around noon. There was nothing anyone felt like doing, so we drove north through the valley, through its white baked badlands with the mountains rising so high on either side, peaks dusted white and dotted with distant green pinpoints of pines. Through this raw beauty we traveled in gloom, hardly seeing.

Driving past the campground and shops at Stovepipe Wells, we found everything closed up because of a fire at the restaurant and saloon. The melancholy scene added nothing to our own low feelings.

The sun had vanished behind the steep wall of the Panamint Mountains by the time the rattletrap minivan was carrying us up the narrow twisting two-lane, and the sun had set again behind the distant Sierra Nevada by the time we reached the Mahogany Flat turnoff and found the van wouldn't get very far on the rough and rocky road. Miserably, we found a flat place to park just barely off the jeep trail and wandered by ourselves with the wind whipping us around.

Tobias finally said, "We should at least have solstice dinner."

The gusts were too severe for even trying to set up the tent on that narrow ridge, so we detached the bench seats from the van and put them out on the ground and all six of us sat inside, forming an oval around a candle and the last scraps of our food from Yarrow. No-one had even thought to stop at the store in Furnace Creek on the way out, and I realized I didn't have a dollar on me. I hadn't carried money for almost a year. At least Celia had the sense to refill our water cans.

But it was enough, that strange solstice meal, as the van creaked and groaned in the ceaseless wind. We divided up the last of the tamales and fruit, just a few bites for each of us, and raised our camp cups filled with water.

The next day we made it up the road another mile or two but saw no trace of B. And by the third day we were sharing the crumbs of protein bars and stale peanuts.

"He is not coming back," I said.

And then I heard crying. It came from Celia, it came from Tobias and Salvatore and Jane and even Nicholas, it came from all of us, it came from me. I walked away and followed the icy muddy road up awhile and then sat down on the cold damp dirt and looked out to the East, across the yellow immensity of Death Valley and the mountains beyond, into Nevada, and I thought, well that's it, isn't it? Where the astronomer pointed, that low haze of light from the Las Vegas suburbs. Where B said the campers were fleeing on that windswept night, to Nevada motels and RV hookup lots alongside slot machine diners and flash–flooded byways. We go east.

When I got back to the sad old van perched lopsided on the ridge with its thin sheet–metal body gouged and rippled and pimpled from unknown scrapes and collisions, the wind had died down and they all sat on the ground as some crackly mystery AM radio station played Shoshone ancestral songs in the night.

"B told us what to do," I said.

"B didn't tell us anything," said Jane.

"We should go east in the morning," I said. How did I *know*? "Across the state line. Where the glow came from."

In the morning we went east. Celia now held B's money.

"He put it in my hand after the night with the telescope," she said. "I didn't know why."

Highway 190 tiptoed down the Panamint Range and opened up all the way through Death Valley Junction and over the low mountains into a honky–tonk stucco sprawl called Pahrump. It was all steel buildings covering tractor shops and evangelical churches and then we hit the main drag with its newer chain supermarkets and Rite–Aid drug stores and the common Southwest landscape of our time, franchise retail and thrift shops and L–shaped strips plopped upon acres and acres of asphalt islands spaced between long vacant parcels of mostly undisturbed sagebrush.

There were tired people on the roadside selling things: off–road motorcycles, camper shells, pit bull puppies, bits of junk spread out on children's fitted sheets in the dirt. Celia stopped and we bought a big metal toolbox filled with wrenches and saws and hammers and fasteners, for ten dollars. As the last signs of this faded boomtown passed by, Tobias pointed to a half–toppled plywood billboard advertising "desert resort living" just three miles to the south. The tract was named Creosote Creek.

N

16

To the community at the Terraces at Mesquite Pass,

Your letter found me in the High Sierra, in a cabin on National Forest land where I've enjoyed peace the many times I've traveled this route. If all goes well, I may deliver this letter to Mesquite Pass myself. The first snows have begun and I should get down the mountain before I'm walled in by ten–foot–tall drifts. Anyway, it is beautiful here and I only wish I had you all here to share it with — I am celebrating the evening meal alone for now, just me and the lucky mice who call this forest house their home.

The cabin belonged to a family in San Jose, from what I've been able to discern by poking around in drawers and cabinets. The notice from the mortgage service company and the county sheriff went up three summers ago, now, and the paper in the dirty window is now cracked and yellow. The back door, next to a woodpile that has served me each time I stop here for a few weeks, has never been locked in all this time. It doesn't even shut all the way, and each year's melting snow has warped the frame a little more, so that this time I had to dig away an accumulation of pine needles and spider webs just to step inside.

But the camp bed is comfortable and the pot–bellied stove heats the room and my food and my tea. The books on the higher shelves have been unmolested by the rodents and insects. Over the past several days I've read a history of the people who struggled to cross this wall of mountains before the days of railroads and automobiles. It reminds me of how little time separates us from the forty-niners. It also reminds me that the frenzied pursuit of gold with no regard for nature is not something we needed social networks and "smart phones" to invent. These so–called pioneers couldn't be bothered to wait out the winter, so desperate were they for the mineral wealth supposedly waiting in the western foothills. They rushed and stomped through the same majestic forests and mountains that John Muir described as the only temples and cathedrals Americans would ever need.

History remembers those doomed parties who came to gruesome ends during their frozen seasons stranded in the Sierra Nevada, but what about the ones who made it? We hear few tales of their fate, because they neither succumbed to cannibalism nor found fortune on the American River.

They became washerwomen and day laborers, they crowded into canvas houses packed tight on land ravenously cleared of timber and flowers. The luckier among them owned shops, worked as lawyers or accountants, and replicated their Midwestern lives as dully and accurately as possible, and all the regal beauty they tramped across made not the slightest impression upon them. It took a wild–haired Scottish mystic to come the other way, from port in San Francisco to Yosemite, to tell these new Californians what they had never bothered to notice on their way through California.

What was B thinking when he reached Telescope Peak and saw Mount Whitney rising over the other side of the Owens Valley? I cannot say, but I do know that he decided then to *walk* across that vast desert and up again, into the sawtooth mountains of the John Muir Wilderness.

And in Creosote Creek, we attempted to build another Yarrow without his guidance. This tract had more houses closer to completion, the water supply branched from the main pipes along the highway, and still our work felt lonesome and unfocused for those first weeks. Who would live in this community? We began to argue over where we should find our new neighbors, and if we had any intention of staying here ourselves.

The old minivan ran so poorly that we feared using it more than absolutely necessary, limiting ourselves to weekly trips to the strip mall and slot machine town of Pahrump, where unfriendly locals stared at us through pickup windshields. A nervous, bug–eyed security guard of about twenty years old once trailed us through the Walmart aisles while we stocked up on essentials such as tea and toilet paper. He was right there behind us until, realizing his situation, Celia faced him with kindness and said, "We are all thankful for your service to this country." He blushed and mumbled something polite and let us be.

I asked how she knew.

"Post–traumatic stress disorder," she said. "I used to see a lot of them when they got back." She had, for an unhappy year or so before we established Yarrow, worked seasonally in the admissions department of a for–profit technology trade school. Her office had often been full of these same young men from the blue–collar suburbs and rural fringes of the metropolis, with the same bulging eyes.

"They don't know how to do anything but radio for the robot planes to drop bombs on mud villages," she said.

I recalled reading in a newspaper that it cost the nation a million dollars to keep a single soldier in Afghanistan for a year's time. And when they were worn out and used up by their masters, they were dumped in a ruined America, scavenging for money to pay rent and keep themselves numb.

Something about this encounter in the dingy superstore helped us regain our focus and remember our mission. None of us are strong enough to go on tirelessly and selflessly day in and day out. We must replenish our souls with daily contemplation and walks in the quiet of nature, our bodies with the nourishment of good food helped up from the soil with our own hands working the good earth, our minds with the nourishment of ideas and fellowship. And we must replenish our compassion even in the face of hostility.

That night — a warm night well in advance of Spring Equinox — we carried our table outside under the stars and celebrated the meal in the fragrant desert breeze. We looked at the halo of yellow light reaching up over the hills from the sprawl to the south and remembered our stargazing night with the astronomer at Furnace Creek.

"The people who need this community are the people stranded there in Las Vegas," Jane said.

After our morning meditation and breakfast, she and I drove the creaking van to the withered downtown and quickly found food banks and day centers for the homeless. Inside one such center, we asked where families might be seeking shelter in this shattered tourist town with the nation's highest rates of joblessness and home repossession.

"In the drainage tunnels," the director said. "There are hundreds in there."

Las Vegas has little in the way of regular water flow. But when the desert monsoons and winter deluges pour down over that vast bowl of scarred dusty earth, walls of roiling liquid come barreling toward the city along with boulders, whole cottonwoods and willows, abandoned cars and dumped mattresses and all the other detritus of an empire of trash. Beneath its boulevards of neon and plastic, Las Vegas had build huge underground concrete river channels to divert the floodwaters away from the casinos and away from the million–plus people who so desperately needed a water supply. Within minutes of a thunderstorm, millions of gallons of fresh water had combined with rock and sand and been washed completely out of the valley. And inside those vast tunnels, we learned on that day, were scores of families and couples and makeshift human arrangements sharing this unlikely and unsafe shelter because they had no other roof to hide beneath in the blinding sun of daytime.

We parked near an obvious entrance to this netherworld — shopping carts, piles of rubbish, wooden pallets and broken glass — behind a hotel resort that looked half abandoned itself. Stepping over trash and pools of stagnant water inside this long subterranean village, we found many people beyond our current ability to help and many others who ran and hid when we approached with our friendly greetings. But within a few hours we had spoken to a number of people who were cautiously interested in joining our community. We drove back to Creosote that evening with a family of four who had been sharing a single dirty queen–sized mattress and two middle–aged sisters who had lost the condominium unit they shared and were huddled with all the belongings they had been able to carry out in roller suitcases.

With the appearance of these needful people and especially the two children, we hoped our new community could shake itself to life. But the family seemed unable to adapt — the husband and wife fought, the children were sullen, and they all bitterly complained during our meals and fellowship about their boredom. They wanted television, they didn't like working in the sun, and the woman began to disappear into Pahrump. A county bus made a few stops each morning and evening at the highway, and at first she claimed to be doing work of some kind, or organizing their finances, one thing or another. She was just sitting in the grubby little strip mall bar between the thrift shop and the fast–food sandwich franchise, we eventually learned. Who knows how she afforded it.

Dolores, the younger of the white–haired sisters, had even grown up on a cattle ranch not far from where the matchstick tract homes of Creosote Creek had risen. What turns her life had taken from that bucolic Western childhood, we never asked. Agnes, the elder, had lived in the isolated condominium with her husband, and when he died Dolores arrived from somewhere unknown. The whole of the American Southwest had become a strange and lonely series of holding pens for the elderly, from the elaborate golf resort developments for those who lucked into wealth to rundown condos and house trailers for the many more who missed out. They were interesting people but also stuck in ways we couldn't accommodate. Both were soon demanding twice–weekly rides to the clinic in the drab little town, where they could get prescription drugs from one of the government programs that never seemed to run out of funding. Neither Dolores nor Agnes seemed to have any interest in the gardening or the kitchen, and their promises to care for the two children never came to pass, as the children stayed close to the father in their stucco quarters at the edge of our single street of improvised, unfinished houses.

"This isn't working," Jane said to me as we made another costly drive to Vegas to seek more families for our struggling community.

"I have no idea what else to do," I said. "This is just what B had us do at Yarrow."

"And now B is gone and who knows what became of Yarrow," she said.

Jane's eyes looked tired and her hair was wild beneath the bandanna she had tied over it, the dry Nevada wind whipping through the windows as we bounced down the two–lane road. I felt worn out and unsure, and I remembered I had ignored the morning walk and the contemplation that so easily cleared my mind of nervous thoughts. Yarrow had felt like a waking dream. Creosote Creek seemed all too poisoned with the dull despair we had supposedly left behind.

That afternoon we searched the sinister tunnels beneath Las Vegas and were threatened and harassed by the troubled souls living in those shadows. We went back to the homeless centers and assistance offices near Fremont Street and took five people back to Creosote Creek with us. I had no enthusiasm for any of them and Jane seemed just as hesitant, but by sundown we were rattling up the highway again, foolishly hoping that we would get different results by doing the same thing again.

I do not want to waste the paper to say unkind things about these people. But our situation did not improve. Even our gardens, which had risen so easily at Yarrow, seemed stunted and unhappy here. Of course we were trying winter crops now, but winter in the desert Southwest just means chilly nights and a very occasional dusting of snow. The days were brilliant with sunshine as always, the nights not too cold, but whether the soil wasn't getting what it needed from our never–enough new compost system or we just didn't have the dedication and joy we felt in Yarrow, we were short of a bounty.

Celia stared glumly at the table one evening and said, "We don't even know what's happening at Yarrow."

And everyone thought, "Has B gone there?"

It was the night before Summer Solstice and we stayed out under the cool canopy of stars for a long time. Celia announced she would go to Yarrow in the morning. Jane said she would go with her, and after the dawn walk and contemplation and breakfast, they drove away.

I admit that I envied their leaving. But our responsibility is to our community because our community brings us peace and a glimpse at wisdom. By the summer, none of the people we had brought out of Las Vegas would remain.

Keep this in mind when the inevitable troubles haunt your community. Keep in mind that you are still the few and not the many. And remember what you have left behind, and be grateful for the chance to start again, living in harmony with the Earth you had ignored for so long.

N

17

To my beloved friends at the Ranchos at Coldwater
Village,

Celia and Jane drove across Death Valley on their
way back to Yarrow. It would've been more direct to
take the 127 to Interstate 15 and then across the
Western Mojave through the wreckage of Victorville,
but they were compelled to pass by the Telescope Peak
trailhead again, even if neither expected to find B.

And so they returned to that rutted mud road and left
the van where we had left it before, and without any
plans to hike to the peak they hiked to the peak on that
bright morning, seven miles of rock and brush giving
way to sparse forest and finally the bristlecone pines, the
oldest living things on the Earth along with their desert
cousins, the Mojave Yucca and the creosote bush. Celia
and Jane made the ascent without fatigue, because they
walked many miles each day and worked outside in the

high desert sun. And a little after midday they rested and drank from the water bottle and opened the rust–colored metal box that held the trail register.

It was just a spiral notebook full of names and dates and the occasional happy greeting or arcane message. Jane flipped through the brittle pages to the week of Winter Solstice, six months earlier, and found the entry by B.

"A clear day," he had written in his looping scrawl. "Mount Whitney looks close enough to touch."

Celia and Jane, leaning over the notebook together, read the words aloud and lifted their eyes to the western horizon. There was Mount Whitney, jabbing the sky with its sawtooth peak, 70 miles away, the tallest mountain in these 48 states.

They ate a lunch of nuts and dried fruit and retraced their path down to Mahogany Flat. A road cut down the western slope through Wildrose down to Panamint Valley, a Death Valley in miniature, the road finally meeting Highway 190 at Panamint Springs, the air so hot that undulating vertical waves of superheated oxygen appeared before objects just out of reach. They paid seven dollars a gallon to fill the tank halfway and bought sandwiches from the café, its swamp cooler struggling to keep the inside temperature at 90 Fahrenheit.

From here the road wound across the last narrow range before plunging into the Owens Valley, the vast alkali playa of Owens Lake shimmering before them, a lake that had covered some hundred square miles, its shores teeming with migrating birds, until it was choked off by the Los Angeles aqueduct just a century earlier.

They drove the last half hour in the massive shadow of the Eastern Sierra, twisting up the edge of mountain walls and finally turning on headlights as they entered the tiny, piney camp town of Whitney Portal.

B was sitting on a concrete picnic table next to a cool blue pond, as if he expected Celia and Jane to pull up at that very instant.

He embraced them both and they saw his parched skin, his hair grown wild. But his clothing and walking shoes were neat and in good repair.

"I thought I might see you on this solstice," he said.

"We're on our way to Yarrow," Celia said, not knowing what else to say.

B nodded and said, "And I will come with you." His small pack lay on the ground beneath the picnic bench, the ragged sleeping bag sticking out the top, rectangles of paperback books in relief. He followed them to the van, far dirtier and dented than the last time it carried him, and took the front passenger seat when Jane offered it.

They drove in silence down the mountain, B apparently content and the women unsure of what to say or when to say it. As they passed through the Western–style tourist town of Lone Pine on the way south, B looked out the windows at the vacant storefronts and said, "It's hard to start a community without people being tied to that place."

"We know," Jane said. "We've been struggling."

"Each community must have at least one family or one group of friends who feel they belong there."

Celia said from the driver's seat, "This would be simplest when they already live there. Look at this town, all these vacant shops and the closed–down restaurants. But the people live here. Most of them won't pack up and leave, not without real catastrophe to push them away."

"What about us? We had no ties to Yarrow," Celia said. "We just showed up one day."

B smiled and said, "Maybe *you* had no connection to Yarrow. Anyway, we will continue to seed communities like we seed our gardens. But it's too early for us to stay in one place. Now tell me about this new community you've begun, in Nevada?"

And so they told him about Creosote Creek, and the subterraneans they discovered in Las Vegas, and all the troubles and hassles and almost nothing about the joys of growing the gardens or the beauty and quiet of the desert.

B listened and was quiet for a long while, looking out at the Owens Valley merging into the Mojave Desert, the sagebrush changing to creosote with distant Joshua trees on the hillsides. Then he asked them, "How can these people love this community when you haven't loved it first?"

They arrived at Yarrow after the meal time, with the common house dark. B walked the desert footpath we had worn into the dry earth and found Nicholas sitting alone in the quarter moon's light.

"You've come back," he said to B. "Well, I'm the last one here. Ursula left too."

Celia and Jane had gone to the house they once shared and found it vacant. The big upstairs bedroom Salvatore and Jane had lived in was a mess, with black plastic garbage bags half filled with clothing and magazines and other junk, as if someone planned to take it all away and then realized it was all meaningless and unwanted. There were cigarette butts smashed carelessly on the plywood floor and dirty stuffed animals piled in the corner.

More was revealed in the morning light: neglected gardens, a car with no wheels left haphazardly in the asphalt street.

"We were overwhelmed," Nicholas said. "There were thirty people here within a week of your leaving. Ursula tried to care for the babies, I tried to get people to work the soil. We were overwhelmed."

"There is no map for our work but the one we draw ourselves," B said.

"I've kind of had it," Nicholas answered.

They spent the day harvesting what remained of the crops and closing up the houses and the water lines. And then B drove them up into the cool conifer shade of the Angeles National Forest, to a small state park campground that had been permanently closed like so many others. But a stream trickled through this pleasant little meadow lined with live oak and manzanita, and they had the entire place to themselves — even the cold–water showers were functional.

Around a campfire that evening, B told them of his time on the mountain.

"I saw a small city of red stone," he said, "carved from the red cliffs around it. Forests of juniper and pinyon on the red hills, green farms and rambling cottages along the creek, red stone bridges crowded with people, a market square busy with children and merchants and violinists."

Celia asked him, "Is this a real place? An ideal?"

B looked at the flames and answered, "Can it be both?"

Leaving all of Yarrow's supplies with Celia, Jane and Nicholas, B told them to rest as he had rested, and that now it was his turn to return to the work.

Not one of them had seen B for half a year, but by the second day they were saying good—bye and watching the beat—up van bounce down the pitted road. They felt nervous and exhausted and crazy, but by summer's end they would be revived.

N

18

Dear friends at Granite Peak Meadows,

It is good to hear the community there is growing and that your fields are full. As I told you when we last celebrated the meal together at your table, we are creating our lives as we live them. There is not a book you can pull off the shelf with the answer to every question, there is no encyclopedia online to solve every dispute or calm each unique situation.

We have our simple rules and they serve us well. That you would love your community and have compassion for all people whether inside or outside your gardens, that is our most basic truth — that is *the* most basic truth. That you would put aside the three poisons and *not mourn* these toxic things, that is all we have chosen to explicitly prohibit. That you would treat the Earth with love and respect, that is the most complete expression of our humanity. Your reward is to simply be alive to these things as they happen, to dwell not on the banal horrors of your past or the uncertainty of your future. Be truly alive each hour, be a living branch of your community, be free from the dull evils that sap your spirit. When your eyes are open, you will see the paradise you were born into.

These are the pure things, and living in your community according to these moral truths will provide the answer to whatever problem presents itself. The philosophers amongst you may want to challenge and question each of these simple human laws, and I would invite you to do so. But do not testify against what you know is right to find an excuse for what you know is wrong. Do not mistake a lawyer's argument for a philosopher's truth. The lawyer wins on a technicality; the philosopher does not seek to win at all, but to come to a correct decision that brings peace to the mind.

Now I must respond to these weird questions you include in your letter. You ask about B and Celia and Jane, seeking gossip I suppose? You ask if Jane, who was married to Salvatore, left his side and joined B? Why did Nicholas and Ursula part ways? Why do you ask these things? Does your mind so quickly go to salacious gossip? On hearing the story of a man who literally gave his life so that you might have a path to a complete existence, do you so readily wish to peek through the keyholes in bedroom doors?

Jane and Celia went to B because they believed they could find him. They found him. Their minds were open to his words, able to discern his movements in ways the rest of us were too confused to comprehend. B did not abandon us. He left us to mediate on what had happened, and what *would* happen. He did not sit in

91

contemplation upon mountaintops to push us into chaos and confusion. He went up Telescope Peak and across the Panamint and Owens valleys and up to Mount Whitney to clear his own mind of refuse and rubbish that had cluttered the open spaces there during the tumultuous times of Echo Park, of the trial and the prison, of those times before the birth of a new courage and a new path at Yarrow.

But you sit there in the beautiful common house overlooking the hills and trails and orchards and think of what, the naked flesh of those who are dead now? Do you want to sit glassy eyed before a screen reading bits of vulgarity and illiterate rumor, with blinking advertisements for hamburgers and pornography? Do you want to pick at the third–hand lust of another and hit the "like" button in your emptiness? What are you doing in our community, then? What vapid error led you to turn from the crowded freeway of your banal struggle and try your hand at the complete life?

Wash these worthless thoughts from your mind. Double your contemplation, increase your walks on the rich grounds around you, go to your friends and family there and plead for assistance in directing your thoughts away from the insipid.

Buried in this mess, you ask for rules of love between couples, of rules for bearing children. You have all the guidance you need for such things. Don't go looking for excuses for your amoral behavior. What are morals? Morals are the moonlight on our nocturnal paths, shining upon the way we know is right.

But if you must have a list to encourage you, I will tell you this much: It does not matter if a woman and man, a man and man, or a woman and woman lie together — as long as they live honestly, and do not try to deceive the community. What business is it of yours? The community is the refuge of the oppressed. How many run to our gardens and common houses to escape tyranny, whether it be the club of a policeman or the cruelty of blood relations?

Tell your young people to love wisely. Tell them to steer away from cheap drama, to live their public and private lives with the same clarity of purpose and transparency of heart. Tell them not to marry until they are truly adults — a girl or boy of eighteen cannot be expected to have the patience and wisdom to spend fifty years with a partner in happiness, let alone have the wisdom to raise children. Tell them to go live their lives, leave their community, find their own way and help others find the way, too. Do not keep your young people when they are ready to go — if they have grown up in a good community, they will take what they've learned to those who need it most, and they will either return when they are ready, or they will create or join another community where the things you taught them will flower again, perhaps in ways you never imagined.

You ask if divorce is sanctioned. Who among you is planning this violence against your beloved? No–one has signed this letter by name, and I wonder if this is the work of a committee. What tawdry things occupy your time there?

If a couple is childless and refuses to live in peace with one another, let them divorce. And send one of them away, or both of them if they have turned completely to narcissism. But those who have children are not allowed to divorce unless there is violence.

The decision to have a child is not to be made lightly — and once a child has been born, it doesn't matter if it was the result of wise planning or plain lust. The child deserves two complete parents. Do not foster it away. Look at yourselves. How long it has taken to see the way, to find your direction on this Earth? It is your responsibility to give your children the wisdom you never had — the love of the land, the respect for its living things, the time for contemplation, the freedom from the three poisons — and not to fill them with trauma because you cannot respect the miracle of life created by two people.

You may say, "Who is N to tell us how to raise a child? Where are his children?"

I have none, it is true. I have been denied the joy of having a family, of having a community to call home. Today I write you from the cramped galley of a fishing boat waiting out the winter storm at Morro Bay. We are trying to reach Monterey, so that I can reach the communities around Salinas and then those struggling around Sacramento. It is cold and damp and I am getting old.

But I have spent many years with the children of our communities, from those first little Guatemalan girls at Yarrow to the twenty babies born at San Luis Rey Estates over one busy season to the hundred smart young people studying music and art and math and agriculture at the school we created from the ruins of that open–air shopping mall in Rancho Mirage. I have seen parents who openly resented the young lives they created, and parents who sought some constant novelty disguised as spirituality while the children were ignored. I have helped raise the ones who lost their mother and father to violence, and tried to repair the wounds when children were abandoned at our communities, sometimes by people who had no connection to us at all. A discarded child is surely better off within our gates than left at a crumbling city hospital or an overburdened homeless shelter, but this is still an unforgiveable crime committed by the parent.

Anyway, I have witnessed enough and helped where I could — and whatever may be new in our way of life, not one of us can improve upon the natural order of parents raising their children. As for those who want children but cannot for one reason or another give birth to their own, our world is still crowded with young ones forsaken by their biological mothers and fathers. We must lighten our weight on this planet, our only home for now. But we must not deny our humanity and the drive to procreate — let those who are ready and able to have children raise up one or two children, and let those who choose not to raise a family take their place in helping raise the larger family of our communities. Even I, a graying fugitive hermit more accustomed now to writing letters than to having fellowship with you at the table or in the fields, have something to offer those who are in the flower of youth.

I will leave it at that, and hope you have the wisdom to make sense of these things, and to clear your mind of the rubbish you accumulated in your old lives. My boat leaves in the morning, if the weather cooperates and the great monument of Morro Rock reveals itself from beneath this dark shroud, and Samuel will leave by land at that time and deliver this letter to you, if his travels go well. The roadblocks and checkpoints have become nearly intolerable, but we will continue to adjust our methods and habits as those who persecute us run through their arsenal of blunt tools. In any case, the salt spray and the barking of the harbor seals and the call of the gull tell me I am alive, here and now.

Be alive where you are now. Be grateful for the peace and plenty you have at Granite Peak Meadows.

N

19

To the community at the Villages at Newhall Ranchos,

We are in danger of losing our own short history. Your letter describes a community of gardens, of meditation and appreciation, of families growing together perhaps for the first time, of the old being reborn and the young finally free to live under the sun, the sun that gave us life.

But how your very community came to be is lost to you. I am glad your letter found me here, so far away from your white stucco houses and wildflower hills. It was B who rescued your neighborhood, which at that point had been decimated by the banking collapse and the property bubble — and by *decimated*, I mean in the original sense of the word. No more than one in ten houses in that rapidly deteriorating new housing development was occupied when B rolled up in that battered old van, the cargo space filled with the basic tools and supplies for turning the parched ground and dead lawns into a never–ending supply of nourishment for the belly and the soul.

What he found were people under siege, literally barricaded within these red–tile–roof boxes on the wide curving asphalt streets, as nighttime brought gangs of scavengers who pulled the copper piping and electrical wiring from the foreclosed homes, and the drug sellers who set up their toxic laboratories in empty kitchens to manufacture methamphetamine and other numbing concoctions. And with the staving, roaming packs of pit bulls dumped at the interstate exit near the charred remains of an In–N–Out hamburger store, it was unsafe to walk outside even in the daylight. What a hellscape we built for ourselves during those last vulgar years.

Knowing he would be facing people with little trust in anything, B adorned the old van with white block lettering on the sides that read, "Community Garden Supply."

By this point we all dressed and equipped ourselves from the bounty within the abandoned homes we saw on the lonesome edges of every city. Never before has such a calamity of poverty and pain been accompanied by such an obscene surplus of "consumer goods" — pots and pans barely used, endless new toothpaste tubes and aspirin bottles and soap bars, pantry closets with unopened packages of flour and rice and olive oil and spices purchased on credit for meals never cooked, garages crowded with boxes of every kind of appliance and electronic device, and of course the closets filled with clothing. And so in those days B dressed himself from a set of brown deliverymen's uniforms he found in a vacant house. He could spend a dozen hours loading and unloading soil and plants or kneeling in the gardens showing people how simple it was to coax a bounty from the parched bulldozer–scraped lots, and his brown work clothes looked no worse for it. Even in times of crisis and toil and need, we can present ourselves with dignity.

And so you can picture B in his uniform, knocking on the doors of the few occupied houses on each block inanely constructed to give a false sense of landscape variety to whatever corrupted planning commissioners approved the tract so long ago. And you can imagine these besieged residents wondering whether to open the door and accept the seeds and soil and implements offered by this stranger.

To better understand the way B worked in those days, I will tell you that this plan was completely his own, whether invented while he was in solitude within the John Muir Wilderness or simply upon seeing from the corner of his eye what would become your community as he steered through the twists and turns of Highway 14.

Our first communities were in distress then, both Creosote Creek and Yarrow all but abandoned during that autumn. B had decided to grow the new communities where at least a few people still lived, where a commitment to the land and the home still existed, and where a great need for security and self–sufficiency could be greatly served by communal gardens and the fellowship of the meal.

Still, most doors remained closed to him. Only three households joined the effort at the beginning — three modest stucco boxes on a single long, kidney–shaped block at the rear of this tract with its single entrance to the wide concrete canyon below that led to the strip mall and the gasoline stations and the freeway, six lanes in all, eerie and all but deserted. The yellow signs clustered in the dead landscaping outside your community looked to B like sunflowers, but they advertised the auction of the many defaulted properties behind the bland plaster sign that read, in pretentious script, The Villages at Newhall Ranchos.

When I last visited you, that ornamental entrance had been turned into a riot of color by your children, from the application of hundreds of mismatched and broken ceramic tiles found piled in the back of double or triple garages long since converted to playrooms and painting studios and workshops. I recall a wild assortment of tulips, too, mixed with the natural bouquets of California wildflowers resulting from that well–watered spring. And upon those steep, artificial slopes where no human had been permitted to tread, there were walking trails and bicycle paths winding down to the canyon roadway.

Everything you have accomplished there is a testament to the good way you are all living now. I do not want to praise you too much and cause a triumphant pride that makes you lazy and obnoxious, but a little satisfaction is warranted because all who have been to your community come away inspired.

B worked for many weeks there, as much on the gardens as on building the trust and enthusiasm of the people. And when he was fully welcomed and even the most reluctant residents had at least acknowledged this newborn community, he brought Nicholas and Celia and Jane down from the manzanita forest and introduced them to your village. It would have looked desolate to those of you who came later and transformed those empty shells of houses into bright, living homes. But you would recognize your gardens around the original common house, laid out by B alongside the strips of concrete driveway and sidewalk, and you would see the new trails being walked into existence in the chaparral hills rising behind the tract where it was too steep to flatten the land for more houses.

Jane and Celia and Nicholas chose a vacant house near the gardens and quickly transformed the grim, garbage–filled stucco monstrosity into suitable quarters. There were so many empty homes that a particularly horrid one at the edge of the development was picked to serve as a kind of indoor landfill, where everything that couldn't be recycled or composted was separated and stacked — a bedroom piled ceiling–high with rolls of moldy, paint–splashed carpeting, another packed with the remains of vandalized curtains and mini–blinds, an entire garage stuffed with widescreen televisions and ancient computer monitors and other electronic rubbish awaiting eventual transfer to an "e–waste" yard where the myriad toxic metals and materials could be separated and, hopefully, reused to serve people instead of enslaving them.

B stubbornly refused to make himself at home, instead unrolling his sleeping bag each night in the soft sand behind the common house, where he could watch the constellations and the planets before sleeping. By doing so, I suppose he made the others resigned to his leaving again. And, in what had become something of a tradition, that is exactly what he did on the next Winter Solstice.

This time, he asked no–one to accompany him. He had traveled to Los Angeles several times in the weeks prior, and he had found not only Ursula — she still did her morning run along the crumbling concrete channel of the Los Angeles River by the old golf course — but several friends and acquaintances from our first community in Echo Park. About a dozen of them arrived in a late–night convoy when the highway patrolmen were occupied with an insurrection along the 405 in the San Fernando Valley. For so many people hanging on in the city, things had become untenable.

And as the original brave residents at Newhall Ranchos saw for themselves that life in this new community was becoming not only tolerable but quite pleasant, the word spread to their blood relations and former neighbors, and that first autumn harvest saw more than fifty houses occupied, so that you could walk for three blocks and not see an abandoned home.

Such was the chaos in the city and throughout the beleaguered government agencies that many months went by without annoyance or interference from outsiders. At most of these houses, water service had been left on, so that the landscape gardeners who had long since quit coming would be able to flood the awful lawns. Vandals had stripped the interior wiring from the vacant homes, but electric power still reached to the meters. The simple convenience of having a few working lights made the choice to move into a dubious foreclosure a little more comfortable. Solar panels had been collected from around the area and were already providing all the power for the common house and kitchens.

Inevitably, your community was discovered by the tax collectors and health inspectors and those who sold permits to grow food and harassed parents to put children into schools despite the schools being locked and boarded up. We bought time thanks to a good man who was in charge of the nearest police substation — this captain was expected to quell uprisings and battle the gangs over an immense region littered with abandoned tracts and crumbling infrastructure, and he tolerated the legal uncertainty of your village because it was an island of sanity and security. The captain never celebrated the meal with us, and he never gave any sort of consent to our activities. But his wife and their little child began to spend days with us, after she lost her own job 20 miles down the highway.

Anyway, the captain was just one person, with just three officers under his command and no sway over the bureaucrats with their citations and court orders.

You put aside the poisons of your old life when you joined the community, but take a moment to remember your past so that you may better appreciate the present.

As our communities have spread, and our ideals have become accepted by many, you may take for granted that your village can grow its food and trade the surplus for your other needs, or that you run your own schools where you teach your children in small groups, in houses on their own blocks. You know that your rooftops harvest the sunshine for all the energy you need, and that you collect the rain and storm run–off for nearly all your water, and that you care for the health of your community by preventing illness through your activities and what is placed upon your tables, and that you bury your dead wrapped in cotton in the meadows where the body repays its debt to the Earth for creating it, but all of these things were not allowed in B's time. All of these simple dignities had been denied us — denied to everyone in our country.

Do not dwell on that past; it is useful only as a reminder of how far you have come in this brief era.

The time will come when you can call yourself by *our name*, when we do not speak of B in whispers. But it is all right that you live in quiet peace now. B told us often, "We are known by our deeds. Let those who oppress us worry about *our name*."

It was the night before Winter Solstice when he gathered us all at Newhall Ranchos, on that cool dry evening after the storm had dusted our hilltops with white. A campfire blazed and the children sat close for the warmth and the beauty. In rings around them sat the adults who made your community come alive — the artists from the city, the suburban parents who had done everything by the old rules and had watched their lives rocking on the precipice, the ones who had been comparatively wealthy, the ones who had struggled in slumlord apartment courts even in the alleged boom times, the cooks from the restaurants and the strong men idled by the collapse, the music teachers and the motel maids.

Crisis had brought them together, these people who had been placed at odds with one another by the very forces that caused the collapse, through their avarice and corruption. Crisis had brought them together, as had happened at our first communities. But like all people, the people who gathered at Newhall Ranchos had each brought a lifetime of habit and belief and superstition and desire to this new village. They had come from a sprawling low–rise metropolis where, from the time of the pueblo, each influx sequestered according to past geography: Mexicans, Iowans, Jews, Koreans, Japanese, Croatians, Armenians, Salvadorans, Russians, Persians, and especially black and white. The Vietnamese had even divided themselves according to the sides their ancestors took in a war across the Pacific that began in the middle of the last century.

They had lived on islands, islands on the land, until the second or third generation had mixed into the larger population. So they forgot the old constraints of race and culture, but they also forgot how to live in communities. How many people called California home, in those days before the crisis? Nearly forty million souls! More than most nations have ever seen, and yet the people lived as strangers, driving alone in their smoke–belching automobiles to distant office parks or banking towers to click things and stare at screens or stand at machines and swipe plastic cards while the multitudes stacked gallons of soda pop and crates of frozen pizza and bales of toilet paper upon warehouse carts. And then they came home by night, slow snaking lines of red taillights and dull rage, to finally lock themselves within their drywall cells and collapse before another screen, in constant fear of illness or the overdraft, in constant search for something to numb the unease. In this land where winter meant nothing more than putting on a sweater, where mosquitoes did not trouble the summer nights, where the native peoples had lived comfortably in flimsy houses of reeds and gone naked under the gentle sun for most of the year, in this preserve we had all become prisoners.

"You have freed yourselves," B said. "You were like a bear in some cruel circus who looked down one day and realized those chains come right off."

The people laughed at this, a laugh of recognition. B paced in front of the fire, smiling back at them, gazing up at the column of thin white smoke disappearing into the sea of stars.

"What you have made here is real and true. You no longer need to beg for work and fear the layoff. This is your work, here with your community. You no longer need to seek answers, because you have answered with your deeds."

B sat on the ground and looked at everyone, and then he said, "You are already in paradise."

Pointing up at the stars, B said, "The astronomers and their robotic telescopes launched into space are all looking for what? *Another Earth.* And of those thousands of planets we find by watching for a flicker in starlight, something enough like our Earth will be chosen someday soon, and we will begin a very long journey, and the destination will not be seen even by the distant descendants of our grandchildren's grandchildren."

The children looked up at the stars, too.

"You are already in paradise. You were born of this Earth, you are made of this Earth, and you are given life by our sun. Keep the solstice, winter and summer. Keep the equinox, spring and autumn."

Now one of the children called out, "Are you leaving?"

B got up from the ground and walked over to the child and asked, "Is it okay to be selfish?"

"No!," they said in a chorus.

"Then we cannot be selfish with ourselves. I am leaving to help start more communities, more gardens, more schools. How is your school here?"

Again, a chorus of little voices: "Good!"

"Good. We will start more schools like this, where your teachers are your neighbors and your parents." Here he paused, looking back into the low forest, and we all heard the *hoo–HOO–hoo–hoo*.

"That sounds like a great horned owl," B said to the children. "See if you can find it."

And they got up and ran to the hillside, loudly saying "shh" and searching for the owl, and B looked again to the adults.

"You are living in the only paradise we have ever had, so be brave and be happy," he said. "Someone is coming who will help keep the court orders and the ticket–writers away; his name is Salvatore. Be an example in everything you do, and even those sent to oppress you will gain wisdom from the way you live now. You hold the new map of the world, and you will help point the way for so many others."

Then B said he would check on the children, and in a few minutes they came running back, jabbering excitedly about the owl they had seen swoop out of the tree, its shadow fluttering across the field of stars. B did not come back.

N

20

To my brothers and sisters at Alohna Crest Estates,

Why are you persecuted? This is a question I've struggled to answer, as the news reaches me of one community after another suffering harassment, eviction, arrest. I have heard your little dairy there was attacked, the animals seized and the building demolished. My ignorance of running such an operation is complete — none of the communities I've called home kept more than a few hens for eggs — but I can tell you why they destroyed your milk and cheese for an audience of flashing cameras and video streams.

You are free from the poison of their channels, but the millions who live around you are still slaves to the screens. The goal of your oppressors is to turn these people against your community, so that they see you not as good neighbors offering another path but as a threat, a danger.

And you *are* a danger — not to your neighbors, but to the boardrooms of those who order your persecution. The threat is not in your few hundred pounds of cheese or your bushels of greens, but in your entire way of living becoming known to your neighbors who sample it through a basket of fruit or a gallon of pure milk from the happy community nearby, where the children are healthy and live under the sun.

By living a peaceful alternative to a sick and unsustainable existence, you have been branded terrorists. Take strength from this oppression.

There is another oppression I want to mention, because your letter spoke of some disagreement with a nearby community, all because you have raised dairy animals and they believe it is immoral to keep any livestock at all.

By all reports, your animals were treated humanely and lived their lives with the benefits of sunshine and pure food and open space we want for ourselves. You do not poison them with medicine, as we do not poison our crops. We have no rule book to consult in such matters; you must use your own conscience to decide if your pursuit fits within our mission. If you are buying or bartering for dairy food and have the ability to care for the animals and produce your own dairy food, I see no reason to condemn it.

And if another community lives without these foods, then they have no reason to raise these foods. Should we splinter into a hundred groups of zealots, with one saying they will eat only red berries and another pledging above all to avoid fish and yet another vowing to never taste an avocado? Is it proper to eat *any* plant food that hasn't fallen of its own volition from the stalk or branch? Shall we purge our stomachs of the living bacteria helping to digest our dinner? What about the yeast living in our bread dough?

Do not drive yourselves crazy debating these questions. Eat in gratitude, moderation and joy. Eat what you know is right and let your brothers and sisters each what they know is right, as long as the food is pure.

When you celebrate the meal with visitors or strangers, offer them the food from your gardens and the bread from your ovens. And when you are welcomed at the table of another, eat from what is offered to you and do this with appreciation. Who wants to sit with a fanatic who rails against the meal that has been prepared and offered? If you do not eat dairy foods, if you refrain from fish, if like most of us you do not eat the flesh of any animal on the land, then don't take anything from that platter. Eat the vegetables and fruit and roots and bread and oil you know will be on the table, be thankful to your hosts, and celebrate the meal you have been invited to celebrate.

It is a strange pathology in some of us, that in finding the way to live we have also found an excuse to complain to our brothers and sisters if *their way* differs at all. And when so many are at the mercy of government surplus trucks and food banks and the welfare card and the barren store shelf, what gall we have to argue over the pure and healthful food upon our table. That is not a celebration of the meal, it is desecration.

In founding your community, you created first by desire and then by practice the types of food that nourish your lives and your souls. B did not leave a list for you to follow, and nor did any of his communities depend upon a strict list of fundamentals.

B told us only to purge ourselves of the three poisons, to honor the solstice and the equinox, to care for the mind with meditation and the body with movement, to grow and prepare our food with joy, to treat human and animal with compassion and love, to celebrate the meal together, and to live in constant awareness that we are in paradise — a paradise that is denied only to those who fail to embrace it.

Anyone who achieves all of this will not worry over what is on the table of our brothers and sisters.

N

21

To my sisters and brothers at Rancho Rialto Village,

Do not honor anyone or any ideal. Honor is a pretty word for prejudice, or a polite term for slavery. You should respect those whose actions are worthy of respect, because we are defined only by our deeds. Tolerate those who annoy you and have compassion for the fools. Do not mistake your own weakness for oppression. If there is no–one blocking your path, the only oppression is inside your mind.

Think of the family struggling with debt or illness, worried about their house, wondering how to pay the monthly bills for video streams and mobile phones and two or three automobiles belching into the sky. They have built a cage for themselves, and they feel oppressed. But who put them in the cage? It is locked only from the inside.

Real oppression is known to us, and has been known to people throughout time. When thugs wearing badges and body armor raid our communities and destroy our farms, that is true oppression. When our people are hauled off to prison on phony claims of insurrection, that is oppression.

Still, you are free as long as you are without fear. They cannot put all of us in prison. So they take a token few, believing we will cower. Instead we move on, to another place where shelter is abundant and we can easily coax food from the soil. What do we care? I remember Yarrow and so many of our first communities, but I don't suffer nostalgia and I don't mourn the villages we've lost.

We found beautiful, bountiful life in the unwanted wreckage of our era, and the beauty and life are found again wherever we settle, because the beauty and life are with *us*, not within the two–by–fours and asphalt lanes of a collapsed system.

Even in his prison cell with that rectangle of sky his only connection to the outside world, B was free. Free of what? Free of fear and free of worry. They told him he would die. That was their punishment, that he should have the same end as all of us. He smiled at their impotent wrath.

You are free when you aren't afraid. It could not be simpler. And yet your deeds are your only belongings, so you must choose when to battle oppression for the good of all, or when you should retreat from oppression. This is the hardest choice we face.

Don't let vanity push you into a lost cause. The wisest army is the one that never faces battle, but wears out its furious enemy. Is a jackrabbit a coward for running from a coyote? No, the jackrabbit is a survivor. There is no Hall of Heroes for jackrabbits who stood dumbly while a predator approached.

In all things, you must have dignity.

Dignity is not one over the other. It can only be touched in equal portions for all. The murdering despot has no dignity in his uniform heavy with false medals, and the petty household tyrant has no dignity in abusing the nanny hired to care for the unloved children. The bully in a Wall Street suit has no dignity, and is the first to leap from a high window when the conditions of his status collapse. The fanatic who kills his daughter for a deluded sense of honor, he sleeps in terror and is buried in his hate. The farmer who crowds his animals in a living abattoir has no dignity, because he has robbed his fellow creatures of *their* dignity. Those who rape the Earth and poison its rivers, they cannot buy dignity with their riches. Those who lead the ignorant in wars of one religion against another, they live out their days stained in blood and choking on bile. The howling moron demanding he be treated with respect will never see dignity.

But dignity is offered freely to all who wake to the miracle of living and the mystery of existence. The one who sees our bright star rising and smiles in gratitude, she lives in dignity. The child who gently takes the spider from the kitchen to the garden and the driver who stops the car to allow a rattlesnake to cross safely, they live in dignity. The worker denied work knows dignity when he walks away from the modern catastrophe and takes care of himself and his family. The doctor who heals the patient without regard for wealth or insurance cards, that doctor walks in dignity.

When you have let the true world back into your life, when you have rejected the dull poisons, when your hands work the soil and your feet step in peace through the wilderness, you are surrounded and strengthened by dignity.

We have stumbled for a long time, but it is through stumbling that we learn to walk.

N

22

To the community at Joshua Springs Summit,

Our stories do not exist alone, but are entwined with the stories from all of our communities. You cannot say, "Our community has failed" or "We were persecuted out of existence." No community is a failure if it was founded on the right principles. No community has been persecuted out of existence, because it lives on in each life it touched — and even when there is no–one left alive who can recall its name, the Earth itself rejoices because you lived lightly upon the land there, in dignity.

This is not to claim that it was easy to abandon Creosote Creek. Of our first three communities, only one lasted more than a year. And when Celia and Jane failed to return from Yarrow, gloom fell over our dusty encampment in that lonely corner of the Great Basin. Finally it was just Tobias and Salvatore and myself, men without women, the last of the nine. We went about our

116

duties, we meditated in the desert and the silence did well for us. But we were not meant to be monks, living in quiet solitude and renouncing the world. We had been called to *change* the world, one community at a time.

Salvatore left first, saying he would return to Los Angeles and attempt to earn some money. Our meager supply had long since run out and we no longer grew enough food to sell tomatoes and greens at the Sunday swap meet in town. We had even run out of tea, and I began brewing "Mormon tea" from the gray–green stalks of the ephedra bushes along the wash. It was tolerable with a little honey, but so was plain boiled water.

Salvatore caught the once–a–day county bus to Las Vegas. We embraced him on the shoulder of the crumbling two–lane, Tobias and I, and stood there for a long time watching the dirty little minibus bounce down the highway, crowded with riders and their belongings. If you had patience, it was still possible in those days to travel to the city or even from state to state, because many rural bus lines maintained a few routes even after the last of the funding dried up. It is remarkable what public servants can do in the direst circumstances.

That evening I went to my bed without dinner, without celebrating the meal for the first time since Echo Park. I lay there in the hot, dry night and thought of my life before. That life was vapid, but its comforts numbed the mind. Anyway, who has such a life today? Those few who still enjoy such leisure do so behind phalanxes of private policemen and locked gates and tall walls, and there is no narcotic, no drunkenness that can numb their fear. I make no excuse for the ghastly crimes of the mobs, but I do comprehend their rage even as I hope for their enlightenment.

As for my own enlightenment, it ebbs and flows like the Pacific tide. It is enough that I know it is always within reach, if I can still my mind and return to the Earth. I am grateful that, most of the time, I can see my own anger for what it is, that I can isolate my disappointments and then set them aside. I can even put aside the envy I sometimes felt for B, for his preternatural calm and easy smile offered to both friends and adversaries.

But on that night when I decided to also leave Creosote Creek, I held despair and I held doubt. And until I set them down, my hands would not be free to return to my work.

When dawn came, I was in the kitchen making a breakfast of oatmeal and dried fruit. Tobias returned from his walk and joined me at the table and I said, "Come with me. We have nothing left to do here."

"Well, I'll stay a while anyway," he said. "Where will you go?"

I told him I did not know, but it had become impossible to lure settlers to our struggling community when even the lonesome desert town nearby was emptying of people. I supposed it was because the townspeople's money had run out — they subsisted on military pensions, social security, emergency food assistance, disability payments, local aid for housing and transportation. Now that these wells had gone dry, desperation sent them away, perhaps to distant family or friends, perhaps to the troubled city in hopes of finding a little work or a little help. The suitcases and cardboard boxes lugged onto the county minibus were evidence of this.

I felt the whole population of the Southwest shrinking — through reverse migration, through death both violent and common, and especially through the lack of children. Even in Echo Park, when I read the grim news on the screen each day more from habit than any need, I recall the first stunned reports of that steady decline. Through whatever methods, people had simply quit having children. Like villagers in a medieval town visited by the Black Death, the Californians were huddling together in terror, burying their dead, and doubtful they could care for more young. The long Western boom had staggered to a halt.

N

23

To the community at Los Osos Country Estates & Resort,

When I first arrived at Newhall Ranchos and saw all that had been created there, it was as if my two years of gloomy wandering disappeared. Here on this high plain in the dry hills upended by millennia of earthquakes and bisected by great highways and aqueducts, a confederation of some dozen neighboring housing tracts had grown into a kind of city — a city of gardens and walking paths surrounded by those hillsides in their spring glory, all orange poppies and blue lupine.

Lacking any nearby buildings specifically built as schools or shops or warehouses and silos for the harvest, the people had chosen the biggest and most vulgar residences for these purposes — as we had always claimed the largest "model" for our community house with its great table and busy kitchen and quiet corners for meditation and reading. In the space of these eight seasons, the community had adorned the big houses according to their mission, so that the large garage doors of the schools wore bright and delightful murals painted by the children, and the more utilitarian buildings for storing canned foods and root vegetables had neat rows of mismatched wheelbarrows and garden tools outside. A house converted to a kind of indoor/outdoor henhouse was a noisy circus, with the chickens running in riots to the amusement of children who stopped their bicycles and tricycles to watch the impromptu show.

I was surprised to find co-operative trade flourishing amongst these residential tracts, with a lively café every block or so. At one stucco house, the proprietors had built a trellis roof from the open garage doors, spreading down what had been the driveway to the busy street. I had always despised those petroleum–plastic white yard chairs that were ubiquitous before the crisis, but here they had been festively painted and were gathered in mismatched groups of two and three around the equally mismatched tables. Wildflowers grew from the soil and jutted from little vases and bottles, and a pair of girls I took for twins sat in the shade playing a Spanish guitar and violin. It was not a festival day.

I sat and looked with something like hunger on the groups of people here and there, some browsing bookshelves in what had been the garage, others busily talking and laughing. The asphalt street itself was unlike any I had seen in any southwestern suburb, with haphazard traffic of bicycles and wagons, people running with leashed dogs and others riding in strollers or wheelchairs, occasionally cleared by an old pickup truck loaded with vegetables or compost or equipment.

The day was clear and already hot, and when a young man wearing an apron dusty with flour stepped to my table and asked what I would have, I mumbled that an iced tea would be very nice.

He brought it a few minutes later, a tall glass of fresh cold tea with a big wedge of fresh lemon, and brusquely said, "That's fifty cents."

Fifty cents! Well of course, the shops would not exist without a form of currency or compensation. Still, I was taken aback. In my worn old wallet that I carried out of habit more than use, I had a little money left from my long travels and the occasional day labor I worked to support those journeys. I put a wrinkled ten–dollar bill in his hand and he stared at it for a moment before walking back to the house–turned–café. When he returned, looking half amused and half annoyed, he counted out my change from a jar of random coins and left the pile next to my glass.

I asked about B. No–one could say which tract he called home, but a woman painting street scenes on an easel in front of her own house directed me to Celia's place in the original Villages at Newhall Ranchos community. The painter waved down a man she knew, a beekeeper who was headed that way, and he led me along the trail wooded with live oak and yucca, through graded hills that had grown wild again.

At a crossroads he showed me the signpost pointing to the twelve or thirteen developments now connected by these bike paths and walking trails and a single–lane service road along the old power lines, for the little trucks that carried things between the farms. The name of each tract was printed in a distinct font upon somewhat faded plastic signs that had been molded to look like white–painted wood.

"I found this myself," the beekeeper said. "In a mountain of trash blocking the creek down there. It was a signpost the development company must've put up by the freeway exit. Had to point all the signs in the right direction once we planted it up here."

Down the slope I saw the land flatten into irregular fields of neat green rows, and the beekeeper pointed out some of his white boxes between the strawberries and the lettuce. I asked how many people called these joined communities home, and he said about one thousand. One thousand!

Celia's street was quiet, and I did not at first recognize the tall woman with long white hair standing on the wide patio paved with random pieces of broken granite countertops. I realized she was in meditation, so I stayed down on the sidewalk and quietly thanked the beekeeper for his guidance.

After a while she called to me and said, "Will you stay there all day?"

She had made the front yard into a hummingbird garden, and everywhere I noticed the little glimmering birds flitting from one colorful flower to the next. Other than this living floral arrangement, the patio was unfurnished beyond the beautifully jagged patterns of dark and light granite on the ground. She sat with her back to the cracked stucco wall and I joined her.

"I never cared for all that granite," she said. "But there's so much of it everywhere! And for some reason, the people who abandoned these neighborhoods almost always took a hammer to the countertops on the way out."

"It's thriving here," I said. "I had no idea it had grown so big."

"B will come around soon," she answered.

I wandered the communities for a few days, finding surprising variation and specialization from one to the other, and upon returning to Celia's patio on a late afternoon I saw her sitting with B and a man in the uniform of a doctor.

B stood and grinned at me and gave me a quick embrace, but instead of asking about the missing years between us, he sat cross–legged again and resumed the conversation with Celia and the physician. They were coming to terms on the use of a medical clinic in an office park down by the interstate. The negotiations were friendly, but I was surprised at the bargaining from B — in the end, the doctor agreed that he and his small staff would be available to the communities in emergencies and on Fridays in exchange for a weekly supply of fresh food for the medical staff and their families.

"And flowers," the doctor said. "My wife insists on fresh flowers. And also honey."

With that, they put their hands together and Celia offered lemonade to everyone.

"The doctor here doesn't like to get his hands in the soil," B said by way of introduction to me. "But he doesn't mind delivering our babies and patching up our bloody wounds now and then."

"My ancestors would die again of shame if I became a farmer," the doctor said. "It's not for me to grow spinach and onions. Anyway, you have a healthy population here. Not too much work for me, right?"

When the man left, B stretched out on the cool granite and said to me, "And that's how we got ourselves a doctor."

"He brought his whole family from India right before the crash," Celia said. "Not the best timing. But he does surgery at Cedars–Sinai a couple times a month, and that's almost enough."

I watched the figure in light blue scrubs disappear around the corner.

"He lives at Tejon Ranch Terraces," she said. "They're one of the few families who actually bought one of those McMansions and stayed here through it all."

"And now the ninth hole outside their living room is a cantaloupe farm," B said. "Come walk with me to the community house."

Celia asked, "Which one tonight?" and B said maybe the Residences at Clarita Falls.

We walked in silence for a few minutes and then I asked the both of them, "How did you do all this?"

"By *not* doing," B answered. "By being outnumbered and outargued and outworked."

"And yet they celebrate the meal and the solstice and the equinox, and they refuse the three poisons—"

"*We* do the things we know are right for us," B said.

"He was surprised to pay money for an iced tea," Celia said. "I told him how it doesn't much matter, with the communities splitting whatever profit they earn from selling our produce and our honey and all the other hundred things grown and made here."

The trail here was wide and paved, with a bright blue painted handrail. It ended at a low–slung condominium complex surrounding a swimming pool with a big glass–walled community room looking over it.

"People live where they feel like living," said B. "But a lot of the older ones like it here."

I could smell the saltwater from the pool mixed with the herbs growing in containers all around the perimeter. One lithe, tiny man was doing laps, while it appeared the rest of this community had gathered inside. B held the door open for us and I was shocked by the commotion inside — music playing loudly over speakers, people laughing and talking over each other, a few couples ballroom dancing together, and a stout man in a straw hat behind a tiki bar like you might have seen in a San Diego backyard a generation or two ago.

"This doesn't look like a celebration of the meal," I whispered to Celia. "It's more like a cruise ship in the 1970s."

B had been listening to a couple telling him something in a heavy Fairfax accent, but he suddenly turned back to me and said coolly, "This is where we are, and it is good."

When we all sat at the long tables facing the shimmering pool, the meal was celebrated in joy and with dignity. On the way back to Celia's, B stopped at the little crossroads and then walked to a clearing where we could see the lights from a half–dozen of the interconnected neighborhoods.

B said, "Salvatore made this possible."

And then Celia explained how B found Salvatore in Los Angeles and brought him to Newhall Ranchos just as the vise began to tighten on those who took up residence in these abandoned tracts. At that time, only a few dozen houses in two adjacent developments were occupied by the community. Another bank had supposedly taken possession of many houses here and sent the usual aggressive inspectors and marshals to clear the homes of occupants. But Salvatore took all these piles of gibberish back to the courthouses in town and simply demanded proof that the bank had any legal ownership interest in these property deeds.

Of course the bank had no such thing; the actual mortgages had been shredded into so many pieces and passed on through so many failed and fraudulent business entities that it was nearly impossible to find an actual person who could rightly claim ownership in any part of the failed developments. This bought the community some time — time used by Salvatore to track down the name on the raw land's title. The man was an elderly Armenian who lived in the San Fernando Valley and had purchased several hundred acres of chaparral in the 1980s, long before the developers broke ground.

And as was so often the case, this man was still owed an incredible sum from a front company that had long since vanished. The man's own real estate trust still had lawsuits pending against the developers. It was through this stalemate of old legal entanglements from before the collapse that Salvatore found an ally and champion.

The man arrived in the back seat of a Mercedes sedan, helped by his sons into a wheelchair, his eyes hidden behind huge sunglasses and his mouth hardened into a permanent frown. He was shown the gardens and the makeshift school and the people patching up the long–neglected tract homes, and after some consultation with his family members he asked Salvatore to come to his side.

"No drug dealing, no gangs, none of that?"

"Just growing food and raising families," Salvatore answered.

"That's good, in this world. You take care of my property and I won't push you off it."

To the delight of the community and the rage of the bankers and lawyers, the old man took a rent of one dollar per year and then paid it back as salary for the caretakers.

"It changed everything," Celia said. "We are not running anymore."

"But still *moving*," B said to me. "Salvatore is everywhere at once now, meeting with the landowners we can find, dealing with the water companies, getting permits for the farmers' markets. And are you back to lend your hands?"

"I am," I said.

"In the morning I leave for Reno," B said. "We have new communities growing there. We will drive after breakfast."

B nodded to us both and vanished down a narrow trail. I watched the trees and brush rustle in the breeze for a moment, and heard Celia laugh.

"You seem surprised by all this," she said.

"I suppose I shouldn't be," I answered.

"There are a thousand people here and another twenty communities like this in California now. It's not like farming, more like throwing a handful of wildflower seeds on a field cleared by bulldozers."

"We're a long way from nine of us at Yarrow," I said.

"B would say forget the nine of us at Yarrow and be with the twenty thousand now."

And B *did* say that, the very next day, during the long last conversation we ever had.

N

24

To my brothers and sisters at Hawk Ridge at Truckee Meadows,

Our simple rituals bring our world into sharp focus — so that the celebration of the morning meal is not some abstract practice, but the celebration of the actual fruit on our plate, the tea warming our cup, the bread on the board. This is all I want to say about the "meaning" of our group meals or festival days marking the seasons, because the meaning is already there, just waiting for your quiet acknowledgement.

And so if I describe our small ceremonies only in passing, it is not to diminish them but to let you know how they frame our days and years in a manner that lacks ostentation or pretense. Let your celebration of the meal be common and comfortable, and let it bring you easily to the community at your table and the nourishment you have all brought up from your Earth.

Now I will tell you of the last community meal and then the last day I shared with B, at the sprawling community he led at Newhall Ranchos. It was his habit to visit a different common house each morning, and on this day we took a predawn path through the hills leading to the furthest neighborhood. As always, we walked without speaking — B some distance ahead of me, Celia at my side, and several sleepy neighbor children spread out behind us. As the brilliant white sun rose over the eastern slope, B was on his knees leaning over a patch of orange poppies. The petals began to open just as the children caught up with us, and we watched this morning performance with smiles on our faces.

"Let's not be late," Celia said, and we all hurried down the trail to what was called the Elfin Forest — a few acres of manzanita and live oak along a gash of burnt–colored soil that had been scraped clean for construction trailers back when this had been a noisy colony of earthmovers and drywall hangers and stucco sprayers. Poppies rose up everywhere on this disturbed ground, because they are quick to populate land hurt by fire or men.

The trailers, or portable offices, had been colonized by seven families. The brightly painted rectangles betrayed little of their former dull duties, with their pretty patios shaded by sheets of plywood and tendrils of wild grape, the pathways dotted with tricycles and other playthings. The common house here was outdoors, just a semicircle of wooden picnic tables echoing the placement of the trailers themselves. A stone oven and campfire circle completed the pattern.

Those who lived in this woodland village were just now streaming back from their own morning walks, and the smell of bread baking greeted me as I took a seat next to B. Teapots and platters of fruit and bowls of oats and finally a crusty loaf on a breadboard were distributed to each group by the four who were serving. We all bowed our heads for a moment and then B said brightly, "Let us celebrate this morning meal on this good new day."

Some of our communities eat in silence, and others enjoy conversation except for the beginning and end of the meal. Those who lived at this small village spoke during the breakfast, which is common when there are so many children.

And so there was easy conversation about chores to be done, who might walk the older children to school in the next village, plans to move a batch of solar panels to the south–facing hillside here, even some debate about American composers versus European composers who produced great works in the New World. But there was one young man determined to engage B in philosophical talk. It was not my community and I had no right to judge those who made this place home, but his manner was strange and I caught Celia's eye at the next table when he interrupted yet again to question B.

"I just don't know how to bring it all down *faster*," the young man said, his long hair hanging in his frantic eyes.

"Enjoy this meal," B said calmly. "What is your hurry?"

"I just worry if it's ever going to *happen*, if they're all going to pay for what they did."

The children had quieted, Celia was now whispering to a woman sitting next to her, and it suddenly occurred to me that this tense young man wasn't part of this pleasant little community.

"What will happen will happen in time," B said. "Our resistance is gentle."

"But it's all lined up against us!" Now the young man stood, veins coiling around his muscular forearms. "If we don't strike *them*, they'll strike *us*."

The color seemed to drain from B's tanned face, and for a moment I feared what might happen next. The whole of the camp had fallen silent.

B did not even rise from his seat. Instead, staring off into the manzanita and brush, he spoke quietly:

"You brought everything you were paid to find here, trespasser. Leave these people in peace."

The man stood there for a long time, and it seemed he wanted nothing more than to be wrestled to the ground and hauled away by force. But when it sank in that he would get no such treatment, he mumbled something vulgar and stomped off — leaving not down the trail, but through the woods and over the hillside.

B breathed deeply and smiled now at those sitting around him, finished his meal and his tea, and ended the celebration with some words I barely heard. We sat in silence again for a few moments, and then the children were laughing and chattering and dishes were noisily collected and it almost felt like the ugly thing hadn't happened.

"The truck is ready," B said to me as the three of us departed. "We should leave quickly."

Celia reached out and grasped B's hand. He nodded to her and then led me away, leaving her at the trail crossroads. I glanced back just before we went over the hill. She looked like a statue to me, her white hair holding the sunlight.

A gigantic residence with three double garage bays
had been converted to a barn of sorts, one side filled
with tools and another stacked high with sacks of seed
and shelves of starter plants in the windows. Outside
were the wheelbarrows and long rows of rubber garbage
cans filled with compost, and in the central garage there
were bins full of potatoes and carrots and onions, along
with old formica–and–pasteboard bookcases sagging
under jars of canned tomatoes and peppers.

The truck was a boxy old delivery van, the smell of
smoking grease from the tailpipe telling me it had been
converted to biodiesel. Inside was the garage–barn in
miniature, with tools and food and supplies that would
— along with B's encouragement and instruction —
help the newer communities on our route survive their
first attempts at feeding themselves. B hopped into the
back and made a mental inventory, then called out for
six of those packed compost bins to fill the remaining
floor space. A pair of blond–headed brothers of about
twelve or thirteen handed the big rubber cans up to B,
who thanked them and then did a quick walk around the
panel van, checking the tires and license plate tags.

I slung my little backpack into the cab and climbed
into the passenger seat. B honked and waved into the big
rearview mirror and we rumbled down the driveway and
through the busy morning scenes of people working in
the gardens, carrying bundles and bags, zipping past on
bicycles, and gathered on porches and corners talking
with neighbors. At the stop sign before the main road
out, we heard a chorus of little voices from the school
on this block, singing *La Marseillaise* of all things.

B honked again, two quick bursts, and waved to the schoolhouse windows. He steered down the potholed feeder road and up the onramp to Highway 14.

"Cheer up," B said to me over the engine noise. "They've harassed us from the beginning."

"Now things are so much ... bigger," I answered.

"If you can hear over all this," B said, "I'll tell you how the communities have been growing."

And over the next several hours, across the Antelope Valley and into Owens Valley and the Eastern Sierra, B spoke as I had never heard him speak before — in great detail and with great enthusiasm, as the parched yellow Mojave with its creosote and Joshua trees faded into playas and sagebrush, while the hazy western horizon was replaced by a vivid, jagged wall of mountain rising twelve thousand feet above the valley floor, Mount Whitney highest of them all.

When you begin a kitchen garden, B said, you might start with high hopes and a handful of seed and a watering can. And then you watch the birds and the ground squirrels eat most of the seed and the remainder blow away, or drown in overenthusiastic watering, and next spring you try some seedlings in an egg carton, and next you're composting the leftovers from the kitchen and putting up chicken wire and unreeling plastic irrigation tubing because you've learned to give everything a better chance, and you've learned that the whole becomes stronger when it's part of a bigger system — so that you're moving the hens through the fields to both eat the troublesome bugs and add nitrogen fertilizer to feed the crops, and you're distracting the squirrels with a nut feeder far away from the gardens, and whatever dies both replenishes the soil again and is replaced by its siblings just starting on the windowsills.

And so the new communities were both strengthened and insulated by their variety and their dependence upon each other, and the distant communities both duplicated this effort and added exponentially to it.

"And the time approaches," B said, "when no single community is essential to the larger body, and the larger body grows without worry that a few cells here and there are always sloughing off."

"But what happens if the communities forget that they're even part of the communities?"

B laughed and said that wasn't his concern.

He drove for another fifty or so miles through the desert, carefully slowing to below the posted speed limit through the ghost towns of Independence and Big Pine, and then he asked me to define a community — what made it so, and how would it be recognized?

"We make use of shelter and land that was abandoned by others," I said. "We grow our food, without chemicals, and we don't eat the meat of animals. We teach our own children, bury our own dead, renounce the three poisons, keep the solstice and the equinox—"

B shook his head and asked me to picture astronauts on a titanium starship, headed for a distant world they themselves would never see, a distant world that would be home to their descendants.

"What abandoned shelter can they use, inside a spacecraft designed by scientists and assembled by robots? What choice will they have but to recycle their dead? What animals would they decide not to eat, hurtling through the galaxy in cramped quarters? What solstice should they keep when they're far from this Earth and this Sun?"

I laughed and admitted these things hardly applied to our brothers and sisters who must one day migrate out from Earth as our own ancestors migrated outside their first narrow horizons.

"Celebrate the meal and celebrate the change of seasons wherever you are," B said. "Oppress no–one. Live fully with each other and live fully in your present. Know that wherever you are able to live, you are in paradise. Know dignity in all things. That is all there is."

"That is all?"

"That is all that *must* be," B said. "Everything else flows from those simple things."

"It is always possible to meditate," I said.

"Yes," B said with a smile. "As long as we have consciousness."

B reached into an open bin between the seats and pulled up a pear, tossing it to me before getting a second for himself.

"Whatever is denied, something else is offered."

I said nothing because I didn't understand.

"We can celebrate this pear."

"The pear," I repeated dully.

B slowed the van and steered it to rest on the shoulder of the lonesome highway. We were far from any trees and the sun beat down upon the desert floor. But there was a sliver of shade, on the passenger side, and we sat cross–legged in the dust eating our pears while our brains and bodies rested from the noise and shaking of the old delivery van.

N

25

To the community at Hawk Ridge at Truckee Meadows,

When I last wrote to you, I had told only half the story. I hope you will forgive the abrupt end; it has become my habit to put a letter into the packet whether it is truly finished or not. And now I have another chance, as our brother Nicholas has found me in my little hideout here in the Panamints.

I write these words by the light of this battery lamp strapped to my head like a miner, as Nicholas snores in the loft of this cabin. He plans to come to you next, and I will let him tell you his plans after that.

As for me, my mind is in the past tonight. B and I had driven out of the Owens Valley and into the piney forest, passing Mammoth Lake and June Lake and Convict Lake and finally the great living moonscape of Mono Lake, its lumpy tufa towers catching the last rays of light as the sun sank behind the Eastern Sierra.

Beyond the meadows of Bridgeport, the two–lane highway winds along the beautiful little Walker River. B had his favorite car–camping spot here along the sandbars, built long ago for the National Forest. The entrance gate was locked with rusty chains, but a path of tire tracks through the brown carpet of pine needles led around the barricade. B steered the van through the empty campsites and backed into the last one, so that the cargo doors opened to the sound of the water tumbling past rock and melting clumps of winter's ice.

Spring comes late to the Sierra, even so far down the eastern slope. The temperature plunged with the sun and I put on my wool pullover and extra shirt and still kept close to the camp stove for warmth. We cooked a simple meal of asparagus and pine nuts over noodles and ate in silence at the picnic table. After the meal, I walked along the rocks and onto the sandbar, the cold shallow water rippling past on either side. The darkening sky and its spray of stars kept me there for some time, my neck craning up until it was stiff.

When I returned to the campsite, B was in his old mummy bag on the ground, having found a more comfortable vantage point for stargazing. I left him to his solitude and rolled out my own bag behind the truck, falling fast into a deep sleep. The police shook me awake around five in the morning, when there was just a trace of light behind the eastern treeline.

I do not remember what they said to me at first. I just recall seeing another three of them standing around B, several campsites over, with their headlights and flashlights glaring. In time they put me in the back of the car, a Highway Patrol cruiser, and took B in a plain police car without lights or insignia. There were no questions, not until they had yanked me out of the backseat and led me to the jail in Bridgeport and put me in a holding cell. What did they ask? Nothing of importance — where had I come from, where was I going, where had I stayed in the months before. Only after I answered these bland questions did they get to the point, which was B. Would I cooperate and tell them his plans? His plans!

"He plans to grow more vegetables this year," I said with annoyance. "He plans to see more people learn to feed themselves and live without fear of job layoffs and foreclosures and hospital bills, those are his plans. He plans to watch birds and hear children singing."

But now I knew where they were going, and I said nothing else that they could twist into the terrible shapes of their designs. To the other questions, the increasingly shrill interrogation about domestic insurrection and violence, I simply said there was no truth in any of that. Finally, dumbly, I asked that I be allowed to go free. They said not yet. I asked if I had been arrested. Not yet, they said.

"Well then," I said, "Please take me and my friend back to our truck, so we can continue on."

The answer was no and that's when I asked to call my lawyer, Salvatore, wherever he might be. The plainclothes policemen — I never knew from what state or federal agency — left me in the little cellblock again, sitting alone at a steel table outside the three cold cells, each of them empty and forbidding, a blue–painted metal bunk bolted to the wall alongside a toilet and sink and small shelf all made of dull stainless steel. The place was without windows and the buzzing fluorescent tubes above made me queasy. I let my tightened shoulder muscles fall loose as I inhaled and exhaled, encouraging the fear to go out with my breath.

Some time later, maybe an hour, two regular deputies came for me. They handcuffed me, "for your safety," and led me to a Mono County Sheriff patrol car outside. Just writing these words brings that cold, fresh air back to my lungs. The sky was heavy with purplish clouds pierced with the rays of the afternoon sun. I had been inside that place for most of the day.

Once we were winding along the Walker River again, I felt some assurance they would bring me back to the campground. They never spoke to me, the whole way, and when they released me outside the rusted gate, they watched me from the patrol car.

I walked numbly through the empty, overgrown campsites, finally hearing the sheriff's car make a U-turn and drive away. Once back to the delivery van, I was startled by the sound of someone inside the cargo hold. I retreated to the sandbar, peeking from behind an immense snag of driftwood and brush until a figure emerged from the open doors, hopped to the ground and stretched his arms and back. It was B.

Calling out to him, I ran along the rocks and nearly twisted my ankle. He grinned back to me and we stood there for some time, in relief.

"They believe I'm an insurrectionist," B said.

"That seemed to be the direction of my questioning, too," I said. "Why let us go?"

"To see *where* we go." He motioned to the van and said, "I've climbed inside and out, over and under. Can't find it. But it's here, somewhere."

"To follow us by satellite."

B brushed his hands together.

"Will we still go through Reno?"

He looked up at the sheer canyon walls still slick with ice. "I won't lead them to those communities."

I started for the passenger side, but B turned away from the truck and walked slowly to the river's edge. He stood at the waterside for a long time.

Exhausted and hungry, my eyelids heavy, I sat at the wooden table to watch the road. But the sun had already dropped behind the mountains when I was startled awake by B sitting across from me, his head leaning in closely.

"They will want to attach my name to the communities," B said in a whisper. "Unless I am erased, our people will be accused and harassed by their association with me."

I blinked dumbly at him.

"You must erase my name from the communities," B said. "What the people have done, they've done for themselves. They made themselves free. They should not be destroyed because of the help they received at the beginning."

"You're going into hiding," I said. "And you want me to erase you from the communities? Those communities live and breathe because of you."

B opened a worn old Auto Club road map on the worn old planks of the table. "Here is what the policemen wanted," he said. "It exists on no device, no screen, no data cloud. Not even Celia knows where most of them are."

It was a map of California and the bordering states of the West, the northern and southern halves on opposite sides. Here and there, in clusters edging the population centers, were scores of tiny dots made with a red ink pen. And in B's tiny looping scrawl next to each dot, a name: Shadow Vista Estates, Goleta Meadows, Mariposa Landing, Cabernet Ridge, Adobe Terrace, Mojave Narrows, Covington Spring, Quail Meadows Ridge, Ocotillo Ranchos, San Luis Rey Estates, Antelope Canyon, the Terraces at Mesquite Pass ...

"You have a hard road ahead," B said with a smile. "You must travel to them all."

"To erase your name?"

"To guide them, to watch over them, to steer them just a little when they lose their way."

I shook my head and said, "That's not in me. I've tried to start communities—"

"They don't need a leader," said B. "Just a quiet hand, a sympathetic ear. You might want to start around Auburn."

He pointed to the semirural exurbs east of Sacramento, where there were red dots both large and small, clustered around the freeway feeder roads. And then, his long fingers moving up and across the map, speaking quickly, he pointed to another group of communities around Redding, another cluster near the south end of the San Francisco Bay, and onward into the deserts of Oregon and the north of Nevada and then he flipped the crinkled map, where great bunches of dots ringed the vast sprawl of San Diego and Los Angeles and the devastated Inland Empire.

Our light was fast fading. B deftly folded the accordion of the road map and placed it in my right palm.

I grasped his hand and asked, "How long will you hide?"

"I don't know," he said plainly. "Goodbye, my friend."

B stood and stepped easily to the truck parked behind me, and I did not look over my shoulder as he started the noisy old engine. The van rumbled over the gravel lane and then around the locked gate, and then the taillights came into view and quickly faded into the darkening trees.

I sat there frozen for some time, and when I finally broke from this trance I saw the meal laid out on table's end, two camp plates set across from one another, a dinner of fruit and nuts and a crusty loaf of bread from the Dutch ovens at Newhall Ranchos, wrapped tightly in foil. A little glass bottle of olive oil was placed next to the bread.

In this way, B had chosen to celebrate our final meal at this place along the Walker River.

When I finished the supper, I sat by the water where B had stood. The stars revealed themselves and the rump of Ursa Major pointed northeast. B had left my pack beneath the table, and I stowed the plates and the vial of oil and the remainder of the bread before following the river and the Great Bear down the canyon toward the state line, just a ribbon of pines between myself and the two–lane highway. When I could walk no more and feared I would collapse into the icy river, I found a spot on the sandy slope that was damp but not sodden, and here I rolled out my sleeping bag, unlaced my boots and crawled inside where sleep took me immediately.

What woke me was not the sun, but sirens. But I had another day of walking before I reached the agricultural fields sprawling out from the river's mouth and draining back into the narrow, mud–colored reservoir called Topaz Lake.

First I saw the wisps of black smoke rising in the hazy afternoon light. And then, as I kept far away from the highway on the stagnant water's eastern edge, I saw the great dark hole and the ruins of the little casino and diner and gasoline station, the empty RV park stretching out along the roadside, an army of fire engines and law enforcement all around, helicopters buzzing in the sky above. Here I crouched in the reedy mud and wept.

This is what they had done to B, the skeleton of his delivery van cordoned off and crawled over by forensic technicians, the ambulances long gone now. This is how they made him into what he would never become.

I thought him already dead, and I turned due east now and scrambled over hills and rocks, and I did not let myself be seen in the first town, nor in the second, and I am guilty of stealing food along the way and staring into old newspaper racks at nighttime crossroads, but the newspapers were not delivered here anymore if they were still printed at all. It was two nights and some thirty miles before I was bold enough to climb through the camper–shell door of a battered Chevrolet pickup truck while the driver purchased a half tank of fuel.

The old man drove slowly, I guessed for the economy of it, and I bolted awake at another fuel stop, this time on Interstate 80, clouds of insects around the vapor lights. Here I broke out into the stifling night and took water and even stepped inside the unearthly light of the minimart and demanded the key for the toilet, where I bathed myself using the sink and changed into my other set of clothes and roughly cut my hair and beard with the scissors on my camping knife. It did little to change my appearance, should they be looking for me as I assumed they were, but it was cooler in this desert heat.

Through this hiding and desperate scheming, the image of the black twisted frame of B's truck seemed burned in my vision. In another day I had stowed away in a tractor–trailer of doomed hogs, and I crouched in the straw while they stared at me with curiosity and intelligence, and when I wept for B during that long bumpy ride over the Sierra Nevada, I believe I wept for those animals too, watching me with their wise and sad eyes.

Not until I escaped at Auburn did I happen upon a television playing the news, inside a taco shop by the interstate where I bought a few dollars worth of beans and tortillas. The people inside — the Mexican matron behind the counter and a couple of laborers eating and a trucker waiting impatiently for his to–go order — paid no mind to the screen. The same news must have been playing for three days now.

But here I gasped and clapped my hand over my mouth, nervously looking around and finding no–one interested in my reaction. B lived.

From the sound of the report, B had leapt from the van, in last–ditch fear or remorse, according to the "expert" jabbering into the camera as a news announcer nodded her head in dumb assent. B was hurt but no–one mentioned how badly, only that he was being held and charged for this so–called attack on innocents, and that the authorities sought a second accomplice who might have also jumped free before the awful explosion.

"Chemical fertilizer," they said. Did they even know what organic farming meant? It didn't matter — it would go unquestioned by the masses that a peaceful man delivering gardening supplies to communities of farmers would also pack his delivery van with ammonia nitrate from a gas–fired factory, to randomly kill working people feeding tokens into gambling machines. It was some time later that I heard the other tale, the eventual version of accepted events — that B had intended to crash the truck into the California agricultural inspection station on the state line. His invented enemies, in this case, were working people paid to stand in little booths asking motorists if they had brought any produce into the state, because of the pest infestations that plagued the industrial farms. This, of course, would show our violent hatred for industrialized food production. And, instantly, our communities that could be linked to B were transformed into cells of violent revolution against the technological state.

But on that awful morning near Auburn, I knew only that B had been made into a villain and that all those who knew him would be harassed and hunted. I packed my food away and left quietly, walking up a farm road that I hoped would lead to the first community I must visit on my travels, my ceaseless wanderings, my journeys without end.

I share this story with you now, only because so many years have passed, and the appetite for persecuting those like us seems to have waned, with so much more to occupy their frantic hours. But I am not ready to write his name, and I am unwilling to even scrawl his initials, and if you find contradictions in my letters then you will have to accept them as either intentional or the honest errors of a fading memory. I take the blame for it, is what I mean.

We do not know where B was put to death. For a time, they held him at the maximum security prison at Victorville in a flat and evil square on the Mojave Desert. There were rumors that he was sent up to Pelican Bay after that, and then we began to hear a little about the military tribunal conducted on some crumbling war base in Colorado. What little news of the prosecution had dribbled out suddenly stopped when that federal policewoman refused to testify against him. And then, on a day unknown to us, he was strapped to a metal table and injected with three poisons as was apparently the standard brutality of the era. And B died.

N

26

To the community elders at the Ravine at Holly Vista Hills,

They have chased me from mainland California, but I am watching from my camp on Santa Cruz Island. I am close enough to see the fires that rise over Los Angeles, the black smoke that pours into the orange sky from Santa Barbara to San Diego. I live now on these transverse mountains rising from the sea, fishing in daylight, walking in the sun, unmolested.

How clumsy and stupid they are, without their satellite in space to tell them where we stand. And how stupid and naïve we once were, to not only carry a satellite locater in our pockets and purses for so long, but to *pay* for the privilege.

How swollen with evil they are, sitting in police cars with mouths full of hamburgers and pornography on the radio. Why did they prosecute us? For what great offense did the state and the nation hurl all of its impotent technological might? Because families might sit together at the table, eating food they raised, living without the three poisons?

During the trial of B — if we can believe the words of that policewoman who claimed to finally see and be repulsed by her own tawdry, banal immorality as B sat there serene in chains and an orange jumpsuit — the government lawyer asked why B hated his country.

"I have no country beyond the family who sits with me at the table and works with me in the garden rows," B said to them. "Why is your government so fragile that people living quietly are such a threat?"

And then, just as we knew would happen when that vile informant fled from the common table at the Elfin Forest, the prosecutor said, "You say this nation will crumble and you will stand over the ruins. That sounds like a terrorist threat, wouldn't you agree?"

And B said, "Is a man who warns of earthquakes a terrorist?"

Every time he answered their jabbering nonsense with an honest question, they sputtered and whined to the judge, who sat there fat and corrupt on his hemorrhoid throne, overruling sanity and sanctioning the official violence of the powerful against the innocent.

They hunt us, the few, because now they cannot hope to stop the many. Would they put everyone in their corporate prisons for growing vegetables, for teaching their children to abhor ignorance and bullies? Yes, they probably would, if the jails would only hold more prisoners, if they could only conjure up more money to construct more of their maximum–security fortresses. So they chase our shadows, even as communities blossom like wildflowers and the people may not even know B's name.

What are the charges against me, today? When Salvatore last argued for me before the federal court in Los Angeles, before he himself was threatened with imprisonment for acting as our legal counsel, that bloated old demon on the bench said I faced ten years behind bars for *writing letters*. Calling for insurrection, the judge said!

If it is insurrection to send notes of encouragement to my own brothers and sisters scattered across the Southwest and trying to live in peaceful communities, then I am an insurrectionist.

They are fragile and afraid. Who knew the bones of the entire monstrosity were so brittle? That it would take nothing more than people without money or power simply wanting to live in abandoned tract homes to grow vegetables and live in freedom from the three poisons?

B was a terrorist, they say! A terrorist! Baking his pies and nursing lizards back to health and carrying children on his shoulders through the foothills, that is what terrifies them now — a good man who shows us another way, a way free of nervous despair and dumb greed.

In all of you, B lives today. In your backyard gardens and quiet houses, in your evening meals around the common table, in your abhorrence of credit cards and the void of the screen, B smiles to you.

Years ago, when the calamity began and so many of you lost your pay and then your homes, where was the government? They shoveled billions of their dollars to the corporations that took your work and the bankers who took your homes. When you cried out in need, you were considered fortunate to get a plastic card that would provide a plastic sack full of processed fat and corn syrup and the bleached blood muck of factory slaughterhouses, perhaps a week of foul sustenance if your children went to sleep with hunger in their bellies, subject to poison and sickness for the sin of poverty.

And now these loathsome scum threaten you with life imprisonment for feeding yourselves and walking, with peaceful steps, away from their failed machine. The day will soon come when the bankers and congressmen will knock upon the doors of our common houses, begging for mercy. I am grateful for the instruction of B, who said, "Open the gates of your community to all who are ready to live as we live," because otherwise I would tell you to strike them down, to fertilize your gardens with their blood.

I hope for my rage to subside. I thirst for your fellowship. It is wrong for a man to hide in a cave dreaming of revenge against his persecutors. Wrong and unnecessary, as they are the cause of their own demise.

N

27

To the communities in California,

We have occasionally enjoyed your fellowship and have traded with you over the years. And while we cannot claim to know you well, we know there is much in common about the ways we live.

Something has come to light in our community, and now we wonder if there might be a stronger tie between our distant villages than any of us here had previously known.

I was just a girl of nine when the man we called Ned walked into our village of gardens and red rock walls. He said he had come from California, but he never said why.

We welcomed him as we welcomed anyone who wanted to share in our ways. Ned was not very useful in the garden or the kitchen, but he taught us many good things.

He taught us to celebrate our meals and to take them together as one big family, and he taught us to celebrate the solstice and the equinox and to know the names and movements of the stars and the planets. He led us in walks and in meditation, and he formed our first school here in our red rock common house after the last classrooms in town closed.

He said only that he had lost his family, so we made him part of ours. Even so, Ned seemed to stand apart from the rest of us. Over the ten years he lived here, he spent more and more time alone, either walking the red rock trails or meditating in the tiny cabin he kept at the edge of our village. But he never missed a meal with us, and he never neglected the lessons he gave us in history and poetry and science. We all loved him as much as he would let us.

Ned became very ill very quickly. His hair and beard were white but he did not seem old to us. Still, by the end he could walk only with our help, and something had caused him to rapidly lose his sight. My dad suspected it was a stroke or an aneurysm or a tumor in his brain, as Ned also lost most of his words in those last weeks.

We tried to bring a doctor from Oak Creek, our sister community, but Ned asked us to let him go in peace. And so we let him go in peace. He held on until Spring Equinox, when we helped him up the hill over our village, overlooking the sandstone formations and cliffs. He sat in the shade of a juniper and told us he would rest awhile, and then whispered that he was content, and that he had been able to live in a paradise — the paradise of Earth, which he reminded us was the only place in the universe where we could live under the sun and grow our food from the ground and breathe the open air, and that one day in the faraway future our descendants would long for our perfect Earth, as they hurtled through the galaxies searching for new homes for their new communities.

When we came back after the noon meal to bring Ned a drink and a plate, he was still sitting cross–legged on the rust–colored ground, but his head was bowed in death. We buried him in the rocks, and we celebrated the equinox meal that night there on the sandstone hilltop, as the clear pink sky gave way to a sea of stars.

I cleaned up his cabin a few days later. Not that there was anything to clean, really. His cot was made neatly in one corner and the table he used for a desk was kept clear, with only a row of books at the back and his reading lamp. There was a pillow facing the window, where he would sit and contemplate the red cathedrals of stone that rise up in the East, and there was his old nylon mountaineering pack hanging from a hook on the wall.

Inside, flat against the internal frame, I found a zippered portfolio full of handwritten letters. I glanced at one and then another and then the afternoon had vanished and my brother was knocking at the cabin door in the twilight.

We took the letters to the common house and began reading them aloud after the meals. And, fearing we would wear out the fragile sheets of writing paper, we carefully copied the letters.

What I enclose with this note of introduction is a complete set of the letters Ned kept in his backpack for the decade he lived with us. While they are filled with wisdom, they are also a mystery to us. We don't know of

"B," and we have never heard the names of the nine or the communities they began. We don't know if Ned delivered these letters to the communities he addresses, and if so we don't know why he wrote out copies for himself. Maybe they were first drafts. Maybe they are the only drafts.

Here at Sedona and Oak Creek and Cottonwood and all of our communities in the high country around Flagstaff, we have been blessed with fresh water and clear skies and little of the chaos that erupted in the cities. It is our great desire to share these letters with the communities in California and beyond. It is our great hope that these stories and lessons Ned kept from us in his life will mean as much to you all as they now mean to us — the life of "B" and the beginnings at Echo Park and Yarrow and the many tribulations the first communities faced. I will be bringing you this good news in person.

It has been decided by the community here that I should travel west, not only to the communities with which we've had contact, but to seek out these villages that have just become known to us in name and are already alive inside of us: Mesquite Pass, San Luis Rey, Antelope Canyon, Ocotillo Ranchos and all the others in this packet of letters. It fills us all with joy that our communities of a few thousand souls in the high Sonoran Desert might be part of hundreds more, even thousands more.

Let this letter serve as a greeting to your community. If my travels have been successful, I will be waiting with my brother Ely and our cousin Anthony outside your gates. If another brings you this packet of letters, then my own journey was not a success. But I hope to sit at your table and celebrate with you tonight.

Johanna
The Communities of Oak Creek Canyon and Sedona

ABOUT THE AUTHOR

Ken Layne is the editor of *Desert Oracle*, a periodical field guide to the mysterious American desert, and host of its companion radio show and podcast, *Desert Oracle Radio*. He lives in the Mojave Desert outside Joshua Tree National Park.

Made in the USA
Las Vegas, NV
11 March 2021

19370429R00095